Judd's Vow

Judd's Vow

A Harlow Brothers Romance

Kaylie Newell

TULE
PUBLISHING

Dedication

For Jane Porter, who's taken me by the hand and led me to wonderful places. There wouldn't be any Harlow brothers without you.

Dear Reader,

Writing the Harlow family story has been one of the greatest joys of my creative life. Over the last two years, Judd, Luke, Tanner, and Maddie have become less like characters in a series, and more like flesh and bone people. It's my hope that they'll remind you of someone you love, or could love, or have loved in the past. Because above all else, their story is about love – the kind that isn't always easy, but that ends up giving life the rich textures and colors that sweeten our days. And our nights.

Thank you for following me on this journey, and for welcoming these siblings into your hearts. Happy reading!

Chapter One

SAVANNAH CASTEELE STOOD outside the small hangar at Bozeman International Airport holding her four-year-old son's sticky hand. The chilly late spring breeze kept blowing her hair across her face.

Shivering, more from nerves than anything else, she smiled down at Wyatt, who had a sucker bulging in one cheek.

He popped it out with a smack. "Are we gonna fly on a plane, Mama?"

"Yes, baby. We are."

"Are we gonna see my doctor?"

"Yep."

Her heart squeezed as she took him in. Fine brown hair, huge blue eyes, the cruel cleft lip that had marked him since birth. Today was the day. This was the culmination of months of fund-raisers, amazingly generous gifts from the community, and working extra hours all to save money for the surgery which her insurance didn't cover. Today was the first day of the rest of their lives.

Savannah looked up again, grabbing her long hair and pulling it over one shoulder. It wasn't just the surgery consultation that was making her nervous. It was the flight to Chicago on a private twin engine Cessna that, to her, might as well be a coffin with wings.

She clamped her jaw shut to keep her teeth from clicking together.

"Savannah?"

She turned at the sound of the low, male voice behind her. She'd been expecting the pilot any minute—someone she imagined would have threads of gray in his hair, maybe a dad paunch, a friendly smile. Someone who would make her feel better about flying, about this trip in general.

Grinning like an idiot, she let her gaze settle on the man in front of them. And all her expectations vanished like dust in the Montana wind. There was no dad paunch. No threads of gray. Definitely no friendly smile.

Savannah licked her lips, reminding herself to blink. Wyatt squeezed her fingers, maybe sensing she needed to be snapped out of it.

"Uh...Captain Harlow?" she managed.

He watched her, his eyes hidden behind a pair of dark aviator sunglasses. That part was pilot-y. But the rest looked more like an NFL linebacker. He wore a pair of faded jeans with a worn leather belt, and heavy boots. A white, Montana State T-shirt stretched across his thick, broad shoulders, which gave way to an obviously muscular chest. His short brown hair was messy and windblown, the scruff on his jaw awakening something in her that had been dormant for a long time. Like butterflies waking up against her rib cage.

It was impossible now to tell whether she was nervous

because of the impending flight, or because she'd be flying with *him*.

He stepped forward, still not smiling. Still not putting her at ease in the least, and extended one huge hand that reminded her of a grizzly's paw.

"Judd," he said. "Nice to meet you."

She shook it, trying to ignore its warmth, its male roughness.

"Nice to meet you, too. This is Wyatt."

Judd Harlow looked down, and this time his lips tilted a little. "Hi, Wyatt."

"Hello."

Savannah was trying not to stare. He was older than she was, for sure. It was hard to gauge because of the glasses, but she guessed he might be in his early thirties. She knew he was a commercial airline pilot for Southwest, and had just moved back to Marietta to help raise his orphaned half sister. He was her best friend's boyfriend's brother, and that was about the extent of what she knew about him. But when she heard that he'd agreed to fly her and Wyatt to Chicago for his consultation and surgery, he'd occupied a special place in her heart. Stranger or no.

She smiled, trying not to be too unnerved by his looks, or the way he stood there so casually unaffected while her heart pounded like a maniac. She could smell his faint aftershave on the breeze, and her belly tightened. "Thank you for doing this," she said. "I really can't tell you how much we appreciate it."

"Not a problem. All ready?"

She nodded, gripping the handle of her bag a little too tightly.

He watched her. "Nervous?"

"Does it show?"

"It's okay. I'll take care of you."

I'll take care of you...

Savannah wasn't used to being taken care of. She always did the care-taking. The one who brought the fevers down, the one who paid for school clothes, the one who worried over doctor's appointments and shots and skinned knees. She was afraid of taking too much comfort in that sentence. But she wanted to.

"Have you flown before?" he asked.

"Once when I was little. But not since then. And Wyatt never has."

He glanced down at Wyatt who was still working on his sucker. "You're not nervous, are you?"

Wyatt grinned and shook his head.

Judd reached for her bag. She handed it over and felt the immediate tingle of blood returning to her fingers.

"It's gonna be fine," he said. "Promise."

He wasn't warm and fuzzy. Far from it. In fact, he was intimidating as hell, but the way he said that just now, made Savannah want to fall into his arms.

She followed him inside the hangar which smelled like fuel and rubber, and where the roar of jets on the runway was slightly muted. A shiny, twin engine plane sat waiting in the shadows. It was snow white with two royal-blue stripes running horizontally down the sides. If she was an aviation person, which she wasn't, she'd say it was beautiful.

"What kind is it?" she asked.

He opened the luggage hatch and put the bag inside. It was a three-hour flight to Chicago and Wyatt's appointment wasn't until late afternoon, so they'd chosen to stay overnight. Judd had only a small backpack, which he tossed next to hers before closing the hatch.

"Cessna 340," he said, glancing over his shoulder.

She was nervous, and when she was nervous, she got chatty. Her inconveniently sexy pilot seemed exactly the opposite.

"Yours?"

"Yup."

"That must be expensive. To own, to operate. That kind of thing." It was absolutely none of her business. But she was having a hard time shutting her mouth, and the sound of his voice was oddly soothing.

"It can get that way. I charter some flights on the side to help offset the costs."

Good. That was good. That meant he flew all the time. For a living. In his free time. Maybe on the weekends. And the more he flew, the more experienced that made him, and the better she felt about climbing into this thing with her only child in tow.

"Mama, I'm hungry."

"Okay, baby."

Savannah pulled their emergency pack of Goldfish crackers from her purse, but looked at Judd for permission before giving them to Wyatt. If the plane was as pristine on the inside as it was on the outside, he might not appreciate cracker crumbs between his seats.

"Please," he said, waving a hand. "Go ahead."

She tore the bag open and handed it over. She didn't think she'd be able to eat if someone paid her.

Rubbing Wyatt's back, she watched Judd walk around the Cessna. His T-shirt rode up as he pushed the vertical door up, exposing a sliver of muscled abs. Not much, but enough to make out a dark line of hair that disappeared below his belt.

Savannah swallowed, her mouth suddenly dry.

He turned and took his glasses off. "Ready?"

She wasn't quite prepared for how he'd look without them. She should have been. The man's body was a work of art, it was a good bet the rest of him would match. But his eyes were a shade of blue reserved for the ocean on a cloudy day.

He smiled, and for the first time, she noticed two long, deep dimples cut into each cheek. He looked so much like his brother Luke that she could only stand there and stare for a second. It had been so long since she'd noticed a man's smile. Since she'd noticed a man's *anything*, for that matter. When Steven had left, she'd had to put her head down and concentrate on raising Wyatt the best she knew how. She didn't have time for dating. The truth was, she gave most of herself to her son, and happily. What was left over was so thin, you could see right through it.

The thought was like a splash of cold water to her face. *The consultation, the surgery, poor little Wyatt...* All of a sudden, the day felt so overwhelming, she thought she might be sick.

"I'm sorry…uh, is there a restroom I could use before we take off?"

Judd's smile faded. "You okay?"

"Fine. Just a little faint."

"Right by the entrance. To your left."

"Thank you." She looked down at Wyatt. "Do you have to go, honey?"

"No, Mama. I went before, remember?"

She did remember. She'd insisted he go roughly a dozen times before they left for the airport.

"Why don't you come with me, then, okay?"

"Okay."

She glanced at Judd, her stomach rolling. "Thank you. We won't be long."

"Take your time."

Savannah couldn't remember the last time she'd been able to take her time with anything. Much less in the bathroom. Wyatt had a habit of telling her knock-knock jokes through the door.

But they always made her laugh.

Chapter Two

WITH THE PLANE facing the runway, Judd put on the breaks and waited for the tower to clear him for takeoff. The propellers whirred on either side—silver blurs in the bright spring afternoon. It was a perfect day, not a cloud in the deep-blue sky. The kind of day when the jagged, snowcapped mountains surrounding Bozeman looked more like a painting rather than something real, something tangible.

The sun was warm through the windshield, and he reached up to reposition the air-conditioning vent. He'd just gone through his checklist with Savannah Casteele staring a hole right through his skull. Even now, he could feel her nervous gaze on his shoulders, and it made him want to turn around and touch her leg. But maybe that didn't have so much to do with reassuring her, and had more to do with just wanting to touch her, period.

She was beautiful with long, silky hair, smooth ivory skin, and curves in all the right places. She was also scared to fucking death. He had a feeling she'd gone to the john to toss what was left of her breakfast before boarding, and he honestly had no idea what to do with that. As a commercial pilot, he wasn't used to offering much comfort to his passengers who were afraid of flying. The flight attendants did that. Judd wasn't great at comforting. He *was* good at touching, but there was that gray area again.

Her kid was adorable, and as well-mannered as they came. When Luke had asked him for this favor, Judd had been happy to do it. But his little brother had left out the part where this single mother and her son would immediately endear themselves, and that had taken him by surprise.

Judd didn't like to think of himself as calloused. He was used to keeping people at arm's length out of simple self-preservation. But he admired toughness. And it was obvious these two had some to spare.

"Two Nine Tango Papa, clear for taxi runway one seven," the flight controller said through the staticky radio.

"Taxi runway one seven, Two Nine Tango Papa."

Judd tightened his grip on the throttle, the hum of the plane's engines as familiar as the sound of his own breathing. His headset drowned out everything else, but he glanced back at Savannah and Wyatt one more time, giving them a thumbs-up. Wyatt grinned, the dramatic V shape of his top lip softening some, and jutted his small thumb in the air. Savannah stared back, her green eyes as round as saucers.

"It's okay," he mouthed.

She nodded, but he could see her hands shaking from where he sat. All of a sudden, he wanted to pull her into his lap. He didn't like that look on her face, or the way her chest rose and fell so fast, like a bird's. He wanted her to feel safe with him.

"Two Nine Tango Papa, runway one seven clear for takeoff."

"Runway one seven," Judd replied into his mic. "Clear for takeoff, Two Nine Tango Papa."

Facing the runway again, he slowly eased the throttle up. The plane jerked forward like an eager animal being turned loose. The hum of the engines became a steady roar as they ate up the tarmac. The tower flew past, jets taxiing to their gates caught the sun on their wings, flashing the briefest of greetings. And then they were in the air, climbing, climbing, and leaving the ground below like a distant memory.

He looked over his shoulder again, and saw that Wyatt was still grinning, looking out the window in wide-eyed wonder. Judd remembered feeling the same way the one and only time he flew as a kid. Like the world had suddenly opened up to its endless possibilities, and he had the key within his reach.

Savannah was another story. Her face had turned mildly green as she gripped her little boy's knee.

He smiled at her reassuringly as the plane bounced through some air pockets, the sun moving slowly through the windows of the cabin as they banked west.

"Two Nine Tango Papa, fly heading two five seven," the tower said. "Contact departure. Good day."

Judd squinted through his sunglasses at the horizon ahead. "Two Nine Tango Papa, good day."

It'd be a nice flight to Chicago. A relatively gentle ride for his passengers and a kick-ass way to spend an afternoon, as far as he was concerned. But knowing the woman sitting behind him was about two minutes from passing clean out, he couldn't really relax and enjoy it.

Holding the yoke with one hand, he turned to Savannah and hooked his finger at her. "Want to come up here for a minute? I can show you how everything works. The more you know, the better you'll feel."

She blinked at him.

"I have an extra headset," he continued above the hum of the engines. "You can hear the tower, other planes. If you want."

She looked at Wyatt again and leaned close to his ear. He nodded at whatever she said, without taking his gaze from the window. If she was planning on using him as an excuse to keep her ass in her seat, it wasn't going to work. The kid might just be a born pilot judging by the look on his face.

She unhooked her seat belt and stood on unsteady legs. Holding onto the seatbacks, she made her way up the narrow aisle, then eased herself down next to him. She smelled good. Really good. Like shampoo and coconuts.

After she buckled herself in, he handed her the headset. With one more look over her shoulder at her son, she positioned the headset over her ears, and moved the mic in front of her heart-shaped mouth.

"There," he said. "Now you can hear everything I hear. Good?"

She nodded, staring at the controls. "Don't you *ever* get nervous?"

"Sure. When some idiot passes me going eighty in a fifty."

"But never in a plane?"

"Flying is extremely safe."

She groaned. "I know. The whole 'driving is more dangerous than flying' thing."

"I could give you some statistics."

"I'm already feeling nauseous enough as it is."

He smiled and glanced out his window.

"Thank you for inviting me up," she continued. "I know you're trying to keep me from losing it. Probably all over your leather seats."

"Listen, it wouldn't be the first time. Won't be the last. They clean up pretty well."

This time she smiled, too. And it transformed her. For a second, he saw the nerves disappear and the beauty rise to the surface. He wondered what kind of woman Savannah Casteele was. But he thought he already knew. She seemed like a good mom. And good moms were usually fairly invested—leaning toward commitment, relationships. He, himself, was good at sex, shitty at relationships. But the kind of women he normally went for didn't seem to mind.

"Want me to show you how this thing works?" he asked.

She made a face. "No. Thank you, but no. I'd rather just talk. Wyatt usually keeps me company, but he seems lost to the magic of flight at the moment."

"That he does."

She wiped her hands down her jeans. Probably sweaty. Definitely still shaking. "I don't know what we would've done if you hadn't flown us. Well, yes I do. We'd be driving. This is so much easier on Wyatt. Thank you."

"Don't mention it."

"You're moving back to Marietta, right?"

He nodded. Judd was private. Sometimes to a fault. His family had a reputation, and he'd left Marietta for a reason. Growing up, he'd fiercely defended himself and his three siblings from the talk that came with living in such a small town. But he wasn't the same person he'd been when he'd moved away. He wasn't so much angry at life anymore, as resigned to the stuff that sometimes came with it.

Luke and Tanner had come back to raise Maddie, their twelve-year-old half sister, after their mother had died last spring. And now Judd was coming back, too. For better or worse. They were going to be Maddie's parents now.

He had no idea how much of this Savannah knew, but had to assume she had the basics down because her best friend was dating Luke.

As if on cue, she took an even breath. "I think it's wonderful what you're doing for your little sister. I know it can't be easy, all of you relocating like this. She's a great kid. Everyone thinks so."

Maddie was a great kid. And as much of a screwup as their mom had been, bringing loser after loser home to live with her, she'd somehow given Maddie a decent foundation. It was going to be up to her brothers to give her the rest.

"Thanks," he said. "It's not easy, especially for Maddie. But I think she's adjusting pretty well."

"And she's living with Tanner?"

He nodded again. "He's got a dog, a nice house. Luke has more of a bachelor pad, and I have no clue where I'll be staying yet, so it just made sense."

"And it's only you?" She shifted in her seat. "I mean, I could ask around about houses if I know what you're looking for size-wise."

"Only me. And I'd appreciate that."

"Sure."

"What about you?" he said. "It's just you and Wyatt?" He couldn't help wanting to know more about her. Who in his right mind would leave these two?

She raised her chin slightly. Maybe the impending answer was something she tried to avoid. And then he felt like a dick.

"Wyatt's dad left right after I gave birth. It didn't have anything to do with his cleft lip. A lot of people think it did."

There was an edge to her voice. Not quite defensiveness, but close. Did she still have a thing for this asshole? It was a distinct possibility, judging by the look in her eyes. Or maybe she was just sick of people insinuating. He could relate to that, but Jesus. If there was one thing he couldn't stand, it was someone who kept letting losers back in when they knew better. His mom had been the poster child for that kind of shit, and Judd and his siblings were still paying the price in being emotionally fucked up—and a little weird, to be perfectly honest.

The plane dipped suddenly and she grabbed his thigh.

"What was that?"

"Turbulence," he said. "An air pocket. Totally normal."

She eyed him, but made no move to take her hand away.

Which was fine by him.

"You're not lying, are you?"

He watched her. She was leaning toward him. So close that he could see a tiny mole at the hollow of her throat. Her lips were a soft, feathery pink, and were parted slightly as if she anticipated a kiss.

"I'd never lie to you," he said.

And then she smiled. Like she believed every damn word.

Chapter Three

SAVANNAH HELD WYATT'S hand as they made their way down the pediatric unit of Northwestern Memorial Hospital. There were brightly colored murals everywhere, statues of beloved children's book characters around every corner. For a hospital, it was a surprisingly cheerful place. But Savannah knew murals could only go so far in easing the fears of its smallest patients, and there was real pain and suffering inside these walls.

As she breathed deeply the antiseptic scent, her ballet flats tapping along the gleaming floor, she had to remind herself that Wyatt was lucky. The surgery was scary, but he'd make a full recovery. There were so many little ones whose recoveries were questionable at best.

This operation was a blessing. And the fact that she faced it alone was okay. Really, it was. Sure, she wished she had a partner to cry with, laugh with, to love her and Wyatt along the way, but she didn't. They'd get through, and they'd be stronger because of it. Still, there was a tiny, insistent part of her that would always long for a father for her son.

Swallowing the lump of nerves in her throat, she looked at her watch. They were already five minutes late. Judd had gone directly to the hotel, where they'd meet later and decide on a time to fly home in the morning. She had a feeling he wanted to give them space, but she wished that he'd come. He was big, solid, comforting. He made her feel safe. Also, he hadn't flown the plane into a mountain. So. There was that.

"Oh!" She looked up at the sign in front of them that offered a list of surgeons. "That's Doctor Lieu's office right there, honey. Room twenty-six. Let's go quick, okay?"

Wyatt trotted along as she pushed open the door to the waiting room. Five or six little kids sat reading with their parents. There were colorful balloons painted on the walls, and a little train running on a track in the corner. Spotting it, Wyatt grinned.

"One second, babe. I'm gonna check us in."

He nodded and she walked up to the receptionist who looked for their names in the computer.

"We actually had a cancellation, Ms. Casteele," she said, glancing up through her orange-framed readers. "They're ready for you now if you want to come on back."

Savannah smiled, anxious. This was it. What they'd come all this way for. "Wyatt, honey." She held out her hand. "Let's go."

He walked over, sweet and obedient, and slipped his pudgy hand into hers. He was so brave. He knew he was going to have an operation, that it was necessary to fix his lip. And he knew that it was going to hurt, but that he'd be okay. She'd promised him that. If everything went like the doctors at Marietta General said it would, he'd have this one consultation with Cassandra Lieu, an expert in pediatric cleft lip repair, then the surgery a few weeks later, followed by a final checkup.

"Ready, buddy?"

"Ready, Mama."

"Ice cream after?"

"Yeah!"

"Okay, then," she said. "Let's hit it."

They turned to a waiting nurse wearing *Finding Nemo* scrubs, and followed her through the door.

SAVANNAH SAT ON the sprawling king-sized bed in the hotel room, watching Wyatt belly laugh at cartoons. They were on the eighteenth floor and facing West, so the early evening sun coming in through the window was warm and golden, glinting off the other buildings nearby.

Her heart was full. Doctor Lieu had reassured her the surgery would be fairly straightforward, and Wyatt would only have to stay overnight for routine observation. As far as cleft lips went, his wasn't a complicated case, and for that she was grateful.

Overall, the surgeon and nurses had been so nice and encouraging, that she'd left the hospital close to tears. It had been a long road, sometimes a lonely road leading up to this point, and she was relieved the end was close.

Wyatt lay on his stomach with his chin in his hands, his little legs waving back and forth. Savannah smiled. She *was* happy. But there was also a strange kind of emptiness that she couldn't explain. It felt like they should be celebrating tonight. Sharing the ups and downs of these last few years, and the resulting outcome with someone special. And they had in a way—they'd had ice cream, and had called Mary and Gran, who'd been waiting anxiously for news. But other than that, the hotel room that boasted every modern amenity she could think of, also felt a little lonely. She was homesick for their small hometown, and their cottage on Church Avenue.

"Come here, buddy." She patted the spot next to her, and Wyatt rolled over to cuddle into her side. "I love you," she said. "You know how much?"

"To the moon and back?"

"That's right. That's the most you can love somebody." She kissed the top of his head. He'd just had a bath and smelled like baby powder. Before she knew it, he'd be too big for baths and smelling like baby powder. But for now, she'd savor every minute. Every kiss, every cuddle.

"Are you ready to go home?" she asked.

"Yeah. But I like it here. They have cartoons."

Kids were easy. Ice cream and cable, and you were golden.

"Where's that man?" Wyatt asked, looking up at her. "The man who flied us here?"

"Flew us here, hon. You mean Captain Harlow?"

"He said to call him his name."

"You're right, he did. His name is Judd."

"He's nice. Is he gonna fly us again?"

"Tomorrow when we go home."

"Do you like him, Mama?"

Chewing the inside of her cheek, she thought about what she knew of Judd so far—that he'd flown them here free of charge. That he'd tried his best to comfort her during the trip, and had been so nice to Wyatt on top of it. And then there was the fact that he was coming home to help raise his little sister, and she knew he probably had reservations about coming home again because of what she also knew about his mother. Most people in Marietta knew *something* about his late mother. But he was here anyway. Out of responsibility. Out of love.

"Yes, I do," she finally said.

And meant it.

Chapter Four

JUDD SAT IN the passenger seat of Luke's Jeep Wrangler as they made their way across town. It was warm enough that they'd taken the top off, and Maddie leaned forward from the back seat, holding Luke's dog, Scooter, firmly in her lap. Her glasses had slipped down her nose, and her signature ponytail was flapping around all over the place.

He turned. "I still can't believe how big you've gotten, kid. That basketball team isn't gonna know what hit them this fall."

She grinned, obviously pleased with the compliment. She was getting tall. But at twelve, she was still gangly and heartbreakingly awkward. He loved that about her. And wished she could stay like this longer. At least until he was ready to let go some.

Scooter, who looked like the love child of Toto and Benji, stretched his neck and tried to lick Judd on the lips. He ducked just in time.

"He likes you," Maddie said.

Luke snorted. "He likes everyone."

"Thanks a lot." Judd leaned his head against the rest and closed his eyes, the sun warm on his face.

"*So...*" Maddie said. "Mary said Savannah might be looking for a babysitter this summer. Will you put in a good word for me?"

At the mention of Savannah Casteele, Judd opened his eyes and looked over at his little sister. There was no denying the tightening of his chest just now. He hadn't seen her since flying them to Chicago last week. He'd been busy trying to get settled, and looking for the right rental had taken up nearly every waking second. Which was what they were doing now. They were on their way to a four-bedroom farmhouse on the outskirts of town. Probably too big for just him, but he liked space.

"What makes you think I'd see her, Mads?" he asked. "I barely know her."

Maddie pushed her glasses up and rearranged Scooter on her lap. "Oh. Well, Luke said Mary said that she's been talking about you. I just thought you guys might be..."

Luke gave her a look over his shoulder. *"Maddie."*

"Well, I'm sorry. You did."

"But I'm sure she didn't want everyone in the world knowing that."

"Everyone in the world doesn't know that. Only you dorks."

Luke and Judd exchanged a look.

"Anyhoo," Maddie continued, "Wyatt's super cute, and I just got my CPR certification and everything. I know Savannah's picky about who watches him. You can recommend me, right?"

"But you're forgetting one thing."

"What?"

"I don't *know* her, Mads. I don't even know how to get in touch with her."

"That's easy. I'll ask Mary and she'll tell us."

"So I can call her up and push my little sister's babysitting services on her?"

Maddie shrugged. "Or stop by her house. Either, or."

"No. No way."

"Why?"

"Because it's weird. She'd think I'm a stalker."

"Only if you like her. Do you?"

Judd raised his brows and glanced over at Luke.

"Hey," Luke said. "I tried to warn you. She likes matchmaking."

"I like people to be happy," Maddie said. "What's so bad about that?"

"I know, Mads," Judd said. "But why would you think she'd make me happy? I'm happy now. Just being home with you guys."

"Maybe. But maybe it'd make her happy to see *you*. And maybe it'd make Wyatt happy to see you. And maybe it'd make me happy to babysit Wyatt."

Judd groaned. He wasn't going to argue with that. Mostly because he couldn't argue with that. He could barely keep it straight.

"What's the address again?" Luke asked. They were on the highway now, passing wide green pastures full of grazing Black Angus cattle, and horses who were shedding their winter coats. The unseasonably warm air buffeting their arms smelled like grass and hay. And a little sweet, like the wild-flowers lining the road.

Judd looked down at the piece of paper he'd scrawled it on. "One eighty-four Chestnut Lane. It should be right past this pond coming up on the left."

Maddie craned her neck and watched a flock of Canadian geese take flight as they passed. Their wings flapped gracefully against the backdrop of the sky which was as vivid as a field of blue bonnets.

"Is that it there?" she asked.

As they passed a small grove of quaking aspen, the property came into view. The setting was movie-screen idyllic—a long dirt road led to the white, two-story house, which was surrounded on all sides by lush pastures and farmland. A faded red barn sat off to the side, a rustic beauty that had probably been there since before Judd's grandparents were born.

Turning onto the bumpy road, they made their way toward the house. He could make out a wide front porch, where a swing rocked gently in the breeze. There was a blue sedan in the driveway, which he assumed belonged to Sadie Mann, his Realtor from Marietta Properties.

"Judd," Maddie breathed. "This is amazing. You could have a horse out here if you wanted!"

Judd smiled. Horses took more time than he had, and the Cessna ate up most of his paycheck after everything else. But she was right—it was amazing.

Luke pulled up to the sedan, where a woman whose long red hair was woven into a side braid waved.

They all climbed out of the dusty Jeep and made their way over.

"You found it!" Sadie said.

Judd reached out to shake her hand. She'd shown him several properties so far, and he felt a stab of guilt for asking her to come all the way out here on a Sunday afternoon. But he'd liked the description of the old place and had known that if he wanted a chance at it, he couldn't drag his feet this time.

"We did," he said. "Sadie, this is my brother Luke and my little sister, Maddie."

Luke shook her hand. "Ma'am."

"It's so nice to meet you," Sadie said. She turned back to Judd, her brown eyes warm and eager. "I think this would be a nice fit, Judd. I really do. It's got the space you're wanting, plus the barn has all kinds of possibilities for a workshop or a spot to keep a plane, or whatever you want, really. It's also for sale. If you ended up loving it, buying it would be an option."

"What's its history?"

Sadie looked down at the clipboard in her hand. "It's the old Tucker homestead. Was built in 1922 and was a working cattle ranch for nearly sixty years before the last of the grandsons decided to go into agricultural science and left Marietta for good. He and his wife moved to Helena in the late nineties." She looked up at him, shielding her eyes from the sun. "It's been in the family since then, though. Mostly as a rental to people they know. At one point it was a bed-and-breakfast, but now it's just waiting for the right person.

The kitchen was updated about ten years ago. It's been recently painted throughout, and the hardwood floors have been refinished. It's just lovely inside. Charming and full of character, which I know you like."

She was right. He had nothing against newer houses. The first house he'd bought had been in a brand-new subdivision in Indianapolis after he'd started with Southwest. It was close to the airport, so that was a bonus. But now that he was older, he found he wanted something different. His mom had bounced him and his siblings around as kids, and they'd never really had a place to call their own. Nothing familiar to come back to after they'd been gone.

He gazed over at the swing knocking softly against the deck railing, and realized this was that kind of house. Where a family had lived for a generation. Where people had come back to again and again. Their true north.

Maddie came up, hugged him around the waist, and gave Sadie a huge grin. Always the charmer.

Sadie winked at her, then eyed Judd. "Want to take a look?"

He slipped his hands in his pockets, feeling the fragrant country air move over his skin like a warm cotton sheet. "I don't think I need to," he said. "I'll take it."

SAVANNAH PULLED WYATT onto her lap. He was rubbing his eyes every few minutes—a sure sign he needed a nap.

They sat in the pretty little courtyard of the May Bell

Center, her gran's retirement home, where flowers grew out of cheerful pots that lined the brick walkway. They came every Wednesday and Sunday, and sometimes on the days in between. Besides Wyatt, Savannah's grandmother was her only close family, and she loved her with all her heart.

"Ahh," Gran said, looking at Wyatt. "Somebody's ready to go home, Mama."

Savannah patted his back, and he stuck his thumb in his mouth, something he hadn't done for a while. She should've taken it out, but she didn't have the heart.

"Gran, you doing okay?" she asked. "You seem quiet today."

Her grandmother smiled, her head shaking slightly back and forth. The Parkinson's was the reason she'd had to move here, but it was a beautiful place. Savannah was just glad the sale of Gran's house had covered everything. She couldn't afford to keep her here on her salary, and her place was barely big enough for her and Wyatt.

"I'm fine," Gran said, shifting in her chair. "Just worried about you."

"Gran, don't. We're okay. We are."

That was true. She was making it. But paycheck to paycheck, and it was nearly impossible to save anything that way. Which was why it had taken so long to get the money together for Wyatt's surgery. If the community hadn't stepped up to help, it would've taken so much longer. The sheer kindness of the people in Marietta never stopped amazing her.

At the thought, she pictured Judd again, and his incredible offer to fly them to Chicago. Her belly flip-flopped like it did whenever her mind wandered in his direction.

"What about finding somebody to watch Wyatt this summer?" Gran asked, her brows furrowed. Her wavy white hair moved over her temples as a breeze blew through the courtyard. Savannah caught the faint scent of her perfume on the air—Violet Petals, her signature scent.

"Remember Mary's boyfriend, Luke?"

Gran nodded.

"His little sister wants to do it," she continued. "Maddie's a sweetheart, and the perfect age. We'd just have to work the logistics out, transportation, that kind of thing."

"That sounds great, pumpkin." She sat back in her chair and watched Savannah with a critical eye. She'd always been able to read her like a book. "But what about you? What about the glassblowing? How's that coming along?"

Savannah's chest warmed. Clerical work at the law office paid the bills. But what fueled her passion, along with every ounce of creativity in her heart, was the glassblowing. She'd managed to take some lessons over the past six months, something she'd always wanted to do. And to her ultimate joy, she'd found she was good at it. So good, in fact, that she'd already sold several pieces at local bazaars and craft shows, and even one at a gallery in Bozeman.

It was Savannah's dream to one day sell her work full time, and build the kind of life for Wyatt that she'd always wished for herself.

"It's going pretty well, Gran," she said. "I'm working on something for you right now, actually."

"Something for my window?"

"How'd you guess?"

They smiled at each other as Wyatt began snoring in Savannah's arms, his small body limp as a rag doll.

"We really are doing fine," she continued. "I don't want you to worry, okay?"

"I just know the number Steven pulled on you, honey. I'm proud of how hard you've worked. It's not easy being a single mom."

No, it was the hardest thing she'd ever done. She'd wanted that white picket fence so badly. But really, she was lucky. She had Gran, she had Mary, her best and oldest friend. And she had Wyatt, the most precious gift Steven had given her.

She leaned forward and put her hand on her grandmother's knee. Her leg felt thin and fragile through her polyester pants, making Savannah's heart hurt. "I love you, Gran."

"I love you too, baby girl."

Chapter Five

SAVANNAH ARRANGED A plate of chocolate chip cookies on the kitchen table and set a pitcher of milk on a red checked dishtowel. She looked up at the clock above the stove. Almost seven. They'd be here any minute.

She'd talked to Maddie about babysitting this summer, and had decided to have her over for an interview after work. Of course, that would really consist of asking about basketball practice and Maddie's favorite music, and giving her all the cookies she could eat.

It was a lovely spring evening, and the warmth from earlier in the week had continued to the delight of everyone in town. Windows were open, lawns were being mowed, flowers were pushing themselves up through rich, damp soil.

Savannah couldn't remember ever being happier to say goodbye to winter. Probably because this summer meant a new beginning for her and Wyatt. Pretty soon his surgery would be behind them, and they'd be able to look forward to moving on. Maybe taking a little vacation in the fall to someplace adventurous and fun.

She untied her apron, one that Gran had made her years ago, and hung it on the pantry door. Running her hands through her hair, she pictured the family vacation she'd always longed for growing up—the dad loading the car, the mom getting the cooler ready and rounding up the kids. She refused to give in to the brief moment of sadness that tried to take hold. She'd always wanted that family, and she'd really believed Steven would be the one to share it with her. But that didn't mean she and Wyatt weren't their own special little unit. They might not look traditional, but the love was there, and that was all that mattered.

Outside, a vehicle rumbled up to the curb. Smoothing her hands down her maxi skirt, she peeked through the sheer white curtains. Her stomach dropped. She'd been expecting Luke to bring Maddie. Instead, it was his gorgeous pilot brother, Judd, whom she saw climbing out of a big red pickup.

Good Lord... Swallowing the sudden bundle of nerves in her throat, she headed to the door and opened it with a smile.

Wyatt came running from behind, and pushed past her to skip down the steps to meet them.

"Wyatt!" Maddie scooped him up and he immediately wrapped his arms around her neck. She was tall and lanky for a twelve-year-old. And cute as a button with her big hazel eyes and trendy purple-framed glasses. Wyatt was no dummy.

"Hey, Maddie," Savannah said, laughing. "I'm glad you're staying a while. Otherwise we might not be able to pry him off."

"Oh, I don't mind. We're good buddies, right Wyatt?"

"Yup!"

Maddie stepped up onto the porch and carried him inside while Savannah's gaze shifted to the man on the walkway. He headed toward her in faded jeans and a long-sleeve western shirt that was rolled up to the elbows. He looked like John Wayne—all tall, broad, sauntering sex appeal.

"Hey," he said.

That one little word was impossibly thick with confidence. Reminding her of when he'd reassured her about flying, when he'd made small talk to get her mind off what she knew would be their inevitable crash landing.

Now, just hearing him speak again made her heart thump in her chest. That smooth timbre was exactly the kind that made women sit up and take notice. That commanded attention whenever it rolled off his vocal chords.

She forced an even breath. The last thing she wanted was to be noticing things like this about Judd Harlow.

He climbed the porch steps, his old cowboy boots thudding on the wood. He'd been in the sun recently—his skin smooth and bronzed, the hair on his forearms bleached golden. She could smell his scent on the breeze—soap and deodorant. Maybe a faint aftershave. Something that was musky and warm, and that made her even more hyperaware. *So much for not noticing…*

Savannah hadn't been on so much as a date since Steven had left. Her heart wasn't the only thing she'd guarded. Her body had been off limits, too. It just seemed easier that way—not to muddy the waters with sex. But she still had a functioning libido that had been denied for a while, and Judd was hard to ignore.

She took a nervous step back as he took a step forward. He looked down at her with a curious tilt to his mouth. God, he really was huge.

"I know you thought Luke would bring her," he said. "He had to work. Hope you don't mind."

"Not at all. I made cookies. Want one?"

He nodded and she opened the screen door. He reached an arm out to hold it as she walked through, and again, she caught his scent.

She glanced at her living room, at the hallway that led to the bedrooms, at the archway to the kitchen, and imagined seeing her house through his eyes. It was small. Actually, that was an understatement. It really was a cottage in every sense of the word. Only nine hundred square feet, one bathroom, a tiny kitchen with Formica countertops that were too small to hold a cookie sheet and a mixing bowl at the same time.

But she tried to make the best out of their limited space with simple furnishings and light, bright colors everywhere. Cute throw pillows helped. Along with sheer curtains, and hopeful plants eager for sun near the windows.

From down the hall, she could hear Wyatt showing Maddie his toys. He was going through a Batman phase.

"Would you like something to drink?" she asked. "I've got iced tea, coffee, soda…"

Judd looked over at her bookcase. There, on the top shelf, was a large picture of Steven and Wyatt. Only so her son would remember his dad. There'd been occasional cards.

Even a few phone calls from Great Falls where Steven's parents still lived, but mostly Wyatt was fatherless. It was a stark reality they'd learned to live with.

Judd put his hands in his pockets, his gaze shifting to hers.

"I'm okay," he said. "Thanks."

"That's my ex-husband. Wyatt's dad. They haven't seen each other in a long time. But I keep it there..." Her voice trailed off. She had no idea why she was trying to explain this to someone she barely knew.

Judd watched her through eyes that could be hard at first, but had definite moments of tenderness in them. Empathy.

"I get it," he said. "I had the same kind of dad."

She knew that. Mary had recently told her about Luke's upbringing. That Judd had been the oldest of his siblings, and had taken his job seriously, even as a boy. Their mom had been a hot mess, something that each man had to come to terms with eventually. In his own way, and for better or worse.

Looking at him now, her heart swelled for the teenager that probably still lived inside his heart. That might always be there to some extent, even as he negotiated his life as a professional. As someone who'd come home again to help pick up the pieces his parents had scattered so haphazardly to the wind.

"Mary said something about that. I'm sorry."

"Nothing to be sorry for. It wasn't perfect, but it taught me a lot." His voice was even, matter-of-fact. "Damn sure taught me what I don't want as an adult."

"And what's that?" She didn't know what she expected. Probably that he wanted to be a different kind of dad. If he wanted to be a dad at all.

"To be giving second chances until the day I die. To be letting people in that don't deserve it…I know that makes me an asshole."

His eyes might have moments of tenderness, but Judd Harlow was a hard man. She guessed he'd learned to be.

"No," she said. "It doesn't."

"My mom…" He shook his head, glancing back at the picture. He didn't finish. Just cleared his throat and looked back at Savannah. And it was as if he'd pulled a curtain over the emotion he'd allowed to show through. It was gone. In its place was a perfectly unreadable expression.

She watched him, mesmerized by his looks. By his stature. By what he might've been about to share. The moment had felt intimate somehow. There'd been a connection between them, because she understood abandonment, too. Her own father had left. But unlike Judd, Savannah had always longed to be reunited. It was why she'd wanted that picture-perfect family. She simply couldn't give up that particular ghost, even though it was buried safely beneath her surface.

"Look, Savannah…"

The kids were giggling from down the hall. Wyatt had gotten his Batmobile out, something with high-pitched sirens. She could hear Maddie playing with him, laughing at something he'd said.

"Yes?"

"I'm not very good at beating around the bush," he said, his voice low. "I brought Maddie because Luke did have to work. But I wanted to talk to you anyway. I've got a few months' vacation coming, so I'm taking it now to get settled back in Marietta, before I start flying in and out of Bozeman."

She nodded, liking the idea of him getting settled. Getting settled meant he wasn't going anywhere soon.

"I just rented the old Tucker place outside of town," he continued. "You know it?"

Her heart skipped a beat. She did know it. In fact, she'd spent the better part of twenty years driving by and watching it age wistfully from a distance.

"I do," she said. "That's a great place. *So* beautiful."

"It's in good shape, but it's been empty a while. The pastures are pretty overgrown, so I'm going to babysit a few goats to help eat them back. Maybe get a chicken or two." He shrugged. "It's mostly for Maddie. She's crazy about animals, and there's enough space for a damn zoo."

She laughed. "I always wanted to live on a farm. It's romantic."

"I don't know about romantic, but there's enough room in the barn to fix up a plane that I've had my eye on." His jaw bunched as he looked down at her. "Anyway, I wanted you to know I'll be around. I can bring Maddie to your place in the mornings, if that's where you want her to watch Wyatt. But I could also have them out at the farm with me during the day. She'd be doing all the babysitting, but I'd be there in case she needed anything. Plus, they could have the run of the place. With the animals and land, it might be fun for both of them."

For a second, all Savannah could do was stare at him. He had no way of knowing, but he was offering an experience that she'd pined for ever since she could remember. She and her mom had always struggled financially. They'd mostly lived in cramped apartments growing up. The place she shared with Wyatt now was the first house she'd ever lived in. The thought of her son being able to spend hot summer days running around a real farm was almost too much for her heart to take.

But Savannah was practical. A realist. And the fact remained that despite how dreamily she was starting to feel about this guy, she still barely knew him.

Maybe he'd read the look on her face, because he cleared his throat. "You don't have to decide right away," he said. "Take your time. If you're comfortable with it, the offer stands. If not, no worries. I can bring Maddie in the mornings, so you don't have to come get her."

"I really don't know what to say." Savannah was used to working things out on her own. Honestly, she'd been prepared for Wyatt to spend his entire summer in daycare. Then Maddie had shown up like a preteen angel, bringing her handsome older brother with her. And he was offering up a *farm*.

"You don't have to say anything. Just think about it."

She nodded, thrown off by a sudden rush of emotion. It was dangerous to be feeling this way. She didn't want to depend on anyone for anything. Leaning in that direction could only lead to heartache—at least, it always had for her.

He glanced down at a small vase on the end table. It was one of her earliest pieces, when she was still trying to get the hot, taffy-like glass to cooperate at the end of her tools. It was rough, but she was proud of it. The colors, a mixture of Caribbean blues, made her think of long days in the sun. White sand between her toes. Going places she'd only explored in her dreams.

"That's nice," he said, changing the subject. Maybe sensing her feelings were too close to the surface.

"Thank you."

"Buy it local?"

She smiled. "I made it, actually."

He looked back at her. "Really?"

"Really."

"You're an artist?"

"An aspiring one. Right now, a records clerk with artistic dreams on the side."

He watched her, a new expression crossing his face.

"Mama, can we have cookies now?"

She startled at the sound of Wyatt's voice. Without realizing it, the room had grown quiet and heavy, a certain electricity sparking between her and the man standing a few feet away. She was grateful for the interruption. If only so her heart could catch its breath.

She ruffled her son's hair. "Of course, honey."

"Is Maddie gonna babysit me?"

Maddie had come into the room too, her Converse All

Stars squeaking on the floor. Savannah realized she hadn't felt so grateful for two people's presence in a long time. Maddie and Judd had brought with them warmth and comfort, something she hadn't known she'd been missing until right then.

"I'd love for Maddie to babysit you." She grinned at the long-legged girl who grinned right back. "If she wants the job, she's got it."

Chapter Six

LOU BIANCI STOOD in front of Judd and Tanner with her hands on her hips. She smiled up at them with a glint in her dark brown eyes, her rhinestone earrings sparkling in the late afternoon sun. Lou was in her mid-sixties, but was the kind of woman who'd be sporting platinum-blonde hair on her deathbed. You could count on it.

"So?" she asked, her voice deep and raspy. "What do you think?"

Judd glanced over at the two goats who were munching grass and looking bored. They were Alpine goats, whatever that meant. Judd didn't know one kind of goat from the next, but they were about the size of two Great Danes and had big, round bellies. One was brown and white, the other was white and brown. He couldn't tell them apart, and their names sure as hell didn't help—Darryl and Darryl.

His lips twitched as he looked back at Lou. "Newhart fan?"

"Bet your ass."

"Where's Larry?"

"That's my ex-husband. Too bad I can't put him in your pasture."

Tanner laughed and Lou grinned, her bright pink lips stretching wide. She was a landscaping client of his little brother's, and her ranch was one of the prettiest in Marietta. Tanner had just redone her massive front yard, complete with a little pond. It was just her taking care of the place though, so she'd had to scale back. Temporarily rehoming Darryl and Darryl was a win-win. Judd would get his grass eaten back, and she'd have two less mouths to feed. She'd even promised to come out and check on them when he had layovers, so it was perfect, really. A match made in goat heaven.

Judd rubbed his jaw. "All right, then. I guess it's a deal."

"You hear that, boys?" Lou said, beaming. "You're gonna get fat and happy."

"I'm no expert, but they already look fat," Tanner said. "How much fatter are they gonna get?"

"Oh, you'd be surprised."

Judd eyed Tanner, wondering for a second if goats could actually explode.

"I'll bring them out tomorrow afternoon, then?"

"Sounds great, Lou," Judd said. "Thanks."

"No, honey. Thank *you*. You're doing me a favor. I don't have the energy for all the critters like I used to."

"Maddie will keep them company."

Lou knew Maddie well. Tanner brought her out to horseback ride periodically, and she and the older woman had grown close. Lou was the fun, eccentric aunt she'd never had, and was the only one besides Francie, Tanner's girl-friend, whom she told about boys. Something Judd refused to acknowledge. To him, she might as well still be in Pull-Ups.

"She's babysitting this summer," Judd continued, slapping at a gnat. "And if she watches him over at my place, the more animals, the better. They'll keep the kids busy."

"Well, bless her heart. Old enough to babysit..." Lou clucked like a mother hen. "I can't believe it. Who's she watching?"

"Wyatt Casteele."

Lou crossed her arms over her bosom, which her denim shirt was having a hard time containing. The buttons strained with the effort. "Ahh. That sweet child. Isn't he having his surgery soon?"

Judd nodded. It was coming up. Which meant, so was another flight to Chicago. Something that he couldn't stop thinking about, to be honest. Savannah was doing this all alone, and that dogged him.

"You know," Lou said, "I'm having a barbeque next week. Why don't y'all come, and bring Maddie and Wyatt? They can ride the horses. Have some hot dogs and ice cream. It'll be fun."

Tanner looked at Judd. "Francie would love it. You want me to mention it to Luke, and he can have Mary ask Savannah?"

That was the thing about Marietta. It was so small, you couldn't really avoid people if you wanted to. Luckily, Savannah was someone Judd absolutely didn't want to avoid.

"Sure," he said, his voice thicker than usual. "Thanks, Lou. We'll be there."

SAVANNAH TURNED ONTO the long dirt road that led to Lou Bianci's ranch on the outskirts of town. It was so gorgeous out here. Massive ponderosa pines stretched toward a sky that billowed with marshmallow clouds. A chipmunk raced across the road, heading for the meadow where bossy wildflowers crowded each other for elbow room.

They were late. Wyatt wriggled in the back seat, barely able to contain his excitement. Mary had given him a pair of chaps for his last birthday, and he wore them now. That and a pint-sized cowboy hat that kept slipping off his head.

She smiled at him in the rearview mirror. He loved animals. Especially farm animals, and chattered endlessly about "riding broncs." If she wasn't careful, she'd raise a cowboy, and then what would she do? Worry. Worry a lot, probably. And then be there to cheer him on.

Her gaze shifted to her own reflection, before settling back on the road again. She wore a little more makeup than usual today. Lou's barbeques were legendary, and this was the first one of the season, so a ton of people would be there. But the real reason she'd broken out the mascara was for one person, and one person only. A handsome, broadshouldered, quietly brooding man who made her want to watch sappy movies and go shopping for new clothes.

She'd shown some restraint and hadn't broken out her credit card yet—instead settling on a pair of skinny jeans with frayed holes in the knees, and a fitted white tank top. She'd pulled her hair up in a messy topknot to keep it out of her face, but had taken extra care with the mascara to bring out her eyes. Gran always said she had beautiful eyes. It was the only compliment growing up that Savannah ever believed. She had her father's eyes. She couldn't remember much about him, but she remembered that. How they changed shape when he smiled. How there were flecks of gold in the green.

Shifting restlessly, she touched the nape of her neck.

"Are you gonna ride the horse, Mama?" Wyatt asked from the back seat.

"No, baby."

"Why not?"

"Because I haven't been on a horse in a long time. And I want to see you ride. That's the fun part."

They turned a corner, and Lou's ranch came into view. It was a lovely place—the single-story house facing the pastures and a small pond where Canadian geese paddled. Several rocking chairs graced the wide front porch, and Savannah could picture Lou there, sipping lemonade in the warm summer evenings.

She looked over at the yard where about thirty people stood mingling. Smoke from the big steel barbeque rolled into the air behind them. The smell of cooking meat made her stomach growl.

"There's Auntie Mary!" Wyatt said, pressing his nose to the window.

Luke had an easy arm wrapped around her best friend's waist, and they looked like a couple straight out of *Country Living*. Beautiful. And very, very happy.

Savannah parked her car underneath the shade of a little cherry tree, and turned off the engine. Before she could tell Wyatt to have fun, he was out and running like a newborn colt toward Maddie.

Smiling, she got out and closed the door. It was warm now, but would get chilly as soon as the sun headed toward Copper Mountain in a few hours. She reached in through the open window to grab her sweater, then straightened when she heard footsteps behind her.

"Hey, Mary," she began. "Sorry we're late. I—"

Only it wasn't Mary. It was Judd.

Savannah's stomach curled at the sight. He looked good enough to eat, wearing a Florida Marlins T-shirt that left just enough to the imagination to make her heart thump. His jeans had the same effect—worn and loose fitting, paired with the old cowboy boots from the other day.

He was holding a drink. Something that had a slice of lemon floating in it. Her throat was dry, but she wasn't thirsty.

"For you," he said. "Francie brought it. Some kind of fruit punch thing."

She knew Francie Tate was Tanner's girlfriend. She'd gone to Marietta High, and was just about the most gorgeous person Savannah had ever seen up close. She was also as sweet as they came, and even though Savannah didn't know her well, she liked her a lot.

"Oh," she said, taking it. "Thank you."

He jammed his thumb over his shoulder, the T-shirt hugging his bulging biceps. "Maddie's gonna take Wyatt out to the pasture if that's okay with you. Lou's mare is bomb-proof. And Maddie will be careful with him."

"Of course," she said, taking a sip of the cool, sweet punch. "I'm not worried." Well, that wasn't exactly true. Thoughts from the drive over came skittering back—thoughts of raising a son who wanted to be a cowboy someday. Who expressed a strong desire to live on the wild side at only four years old.

A cool breeze blew against her face, and she was grateful. Taking another sip of punch, she looked up over the rim of her glass. He was gazing back in that way she found unsettling. His eyes were so blue, so deep, that it was hard not to be taken in by them.

"Have you thought any more about the farm?" he asked.

She crunched a small piece of ice, and it took a second to realize what he was talking about. *The farm…the farm…* Oh, yes. The almost perfect babysitting scenario that he'd presented the other day. Like some kind of hot, alpha, Mary Poppins.

She'd thought about it a lot. The truth was, she didn't know Judd very well. But most everyone in town did, and they liked and trusted him. And Wyatt *loved* Maddie. If it wasn't a good fit, she'd know the first day, and she'd just say so. But she didn't think it would come to that. In fact, she worried how she'd ever tear Wyatt away in the evenings.

Judd started walking toward the yard where everyone was gathered. Their laughter floated through the trees and the tall prairie grass surrounding the pastures. Overhead, a hawk cried, lamenting the world below.

Savannah fell into step beside him, aware that he'd short-ened his steps to accommodate her. He was so big, so tall, that his legs ate up the ground at even a slow pace.

She cleared her throat. "I have," she said. "Wyatt would absolutely love it. He adores Maddie."

"The feeling's mutual. She's pretty good at mothering. Not sure where she got it, since she was basically raised by dudes."

Smiling, Savannah looked over. His profile was strong, his jaw peppered with dark stubble. His hair was longer than when she'd seen him last, and a little messy—something that only added to his sex appeal.

"I think it's wonderful what you and your brothers are doing," she said.

He didn't look at her. Just kept walking with his head down, studying the ground. The muscles in his jaw were working, though. Overtime. "Anyone would do the same."

"That's where you're wrong, Judd."

Then he did look over. Maybe it had been the sound of her voice. Or maybe he'd noticed it was the first time she'd used his name in conversation.

"Mary told me your aunt was going to take her," she continued. "And you guys got her back. Made the decision to raise her. That's not something a lot of men would do. Who are established in their careers, who are bachelors. It's...it's..." She didn't know how to finish. *It's not what my own father would've done?* And maybe that was it right there. The realization that Judd was the kind of man she always hoped was out there, but since Steven, had been too afraid to think about.

At that, Judd stopped and turned. "Maybe it's not something a lot of men you know would do."

She stared up at him. It was a gentle correction. One little sentence that made her wonder if she'd had it wrong this whole time.

Chapter Seven

JUDD TOOK ANOTHER drink of his beer. Something dark and smooth. It felt good going down. Cool in the warmth of the afternoon.

Francie stood next to him, telling him about the renovations on her little house on Bramble Lane, something he'd normally be interested in. When he wasn't flying, he liked to fix things, build things. Which was one of the reasons for the vintage plane sitting in his barn now.

But this afternoon, he was having trouble concentrating on anything other than the slender woman across the lawn who'd just answered her phone and had her back to them now.

Francie swirled the ice around in her glass and frowned. "I don't know whether to go with Pergo or hardwood. I think the hardwood goes with the period of the house better. But the Pergo is so durable. I don't know. What do you think?"

His gaze shifted from Francie back to Savannah. Specifically back to Savannah's ass. He couldn't help it.

"Judd?"

"Mmm."

"Are you listening?"

"Pergo or hardwood."

Francie followed his line of vision, and she smiled slowly. "Ahh. I get it. Floors, schmoors."

"Hardwood," he grumbled, and took another swallow of his beer.

Francie cocked her blonde head, her lips puckered. Like she knew exactly what he was thinking. Which, hell. She probably did.

"You like her?" she asked casually.

"What? No."

"Why not? She's adorable."

He gave her a look. She was almost as bad as Maddie. "Because. I don't know."

"Hmm." She took another dainty sip of lemonade. "I don't believe that."

"Francie…"

"Judd…"

Mary walked up with a huge burger in one hand, and a Coke in the other. "What are we talking about?"

Judd's neck heated. "Nothing."

Francie laughed.

God. This was junior high.

"What?" Mary asked, looking back and forth between them.

"She thinks I've got the hots for your best friend."

Mary's gray eyes widened. "Do you?"

"Jesus. I'm just trying to enjoy my beer over here."

"We know," Francie said. "That's why we came over.

Sometimes you need to be forced into conversation."

"I'm sociable."

The two women exchanged a look.

"I *am*."

They stared at him, and he took another grumpy drink.

Francie reached up and touched his arm. "I'm sorry. You know we love you. That's why I was hoping you'd go talk to her. She's so sweet."

"You act like I'm looking for some kind of *thing* with someone. Which, Jesus, Fran, you should know by now, I'm not." Even so, his gaze shifted over to Savannah again, to the graceful curve of her neck. At the watchful way she kept looking over at her son and Maddie in the pasture. She was sweet. Too sweet for him. "Besides, she's on the phone. She's busy."

Mary sighed. "She could use a nice guy for once. That's her ex she's talking to, and he's a stage four asshole on the asshole scale of assholes."

Judd's throat felt tight. He'd gathered as much. He also thought the guy was out of the picture. Not that it was any of his damn business anyway.

"Say what you really mean, Mary," Francie said.

"Okay. Stage five asshole."

"He disappeared on them, didn't he?" Francie asked. "Just up and left?"

Mary nodded, taking a sip of Coke and narrowing her eyes at her best friend, who was now pacing back and forth, holding the phone close to her ear. "He still calls every now and then. He probably found out Wyatt's surgery is in a few weeks, so maybe this is his way of trying or something. Whatever."

She looked up at Judd then, her short, dark hair framing her pretty face. "I just want her to be happy, you know?"

He smiled, ignoring the way his free hand wanted to curl into a fist. He thought of his own dad. The abandonment still stung like table salt in an open wound. Never stopped stinging, no matter how old he got.

"I get it," he said. "She's family. You look out for family."

"Yes. That."

His gaze slid back to Savannah, where it seemed destined to be. She was now studying her feet, chewing on her bottom lip. She looked sad. Maybe a little torn.

And he wanted to pull her into his arms.

SAVANNAH SAT WITH her gran in the retirement home's courtyard. She didn't have Wyatt with her today. He was out at Judd's farm for a few hours as a test run to see how comfortable her son would be spending time there.

Maddie had been thrilled for a practice babysitting day, and had wasted no time in swooping Wyatt up and carrying him over to the fence, where two rotund goats stood bleating for treats.

Gran took Savannah's hand in her own. The sun was warm today, but not as warm as it had been in the last week, and Savannah guessed she'd need her jacket when she picked

Wyatt up tonight.

"Something's on your mind, pumpkin," Gran said. "What is it?"

She smiled at her grandmother, liking how she looked today. Her cheeks were pink and her hair freshly done. "They called with an exact date for the surgery. Two weeks from tomorrow."

Gran's eyebrows rose, her wrinkles multiplying tenfold. "That's soon. Are you ready?"

"We are. As ready as we'll ever be. Wyatt doesn't seem scared, he's just excited to fly to Chicago again. He loved that part. And they keep saying the surgery is pretty straightforward, so I'm not as nervous as I was."

"That's good. That's real good." Gran watched her. "But there's more. What is it?"

The scent of roses wafted over in the slight breeze, mingling with Gran's perfume. This really was Savannah's happy place. Where she didn't always have to be a single mom, but got to revert back to childhood a little. Here, she got to be a girl again, if only for a few minutes at a time.

She licked her lips, knowing what she was about to say wouldn't go over well.

"I heard from Steven a few days ago."

Gran stiffened. "Oh?"

"I know. But I think he's actually making an effort this time."

"Hmm."

"You know how I feel about Wyatt having some kind of relationship with his dad, Gran. It's important to me."

"Yes, but I don't trust him. Never have."

Everyone had tried to warn her away from Steven and his recklessness in high school. His complete inability to stick it out for any meaningful period of time. But she'd been young and in love, and nobody could tell her anything. Now, she just wished she'd listened. Of course, if she had, she wouldn't have Wyatt now.

"I know," she said, her voice low.

"I just worry about you. I understand you wanting Wyatt's father in his life. I only wish it didn't have to be Steven."

"But it is Steven. For better or worse."

Gran looked over at the purple mountains in the distance. Her hand shook a little, but it steadied when Savannah squeezed it. "So...what'd he say?"

"He said he wants to come out after the surgery and see us. He said he's hoping for a fresh start." Savanna shrugged. "Whatever that means."

"It means he wants to try and get you back, honey. That's what it means."

"Or that he wants to get to know his son."

Gran looked skeptical. "You were so devastated when he left. Remember?"

"How could I forget?"

"Well, be prudent, then. That's all I'm saying."

It was good advice. But no matter how hard she tried to bury the sharp memory of Steven walking out the door, she still couldn't help wondering if he'd end up wanting them after all. Not that she'd ever take him back. She wouldn't. It was just that damn ache that refused to go away—the ache of wanting a whole family. She'd had one for a short time. Such a short, precious time. And then the reality and responsibility of that family had seeped in for her young, immature husband, and he'd left town as if the law was after him. That fast. Like the snap of a finger.

But now he seemed to be finally growing up. Maybe his conscience had caught up to him. Maybe karma had. Whatever the reason, he'd been thinking of Wyatt more and more. And his calls, his sudden interest, was all stirring up the memory of her own father leaving. Had he ever wanted to come back? Would her mother have let him? And if she hadn't, would Savannah have forgiven her for that? It was only speculation of course, because he'd never stepped foot inside Marietta again. Leaving her gutted and a little broken inside.

"So tell me about this farm," Gran said, changing the subject. "Maddie's going to be watching Wyatt there?"

Savannah suddenly pictured her son running through the sunflowers that grew along the dirt road leading up to the farmhouse. It was like a painting out there. Something he'd probably remember his entire life.

"Oh, Gran. It's just beautiful. There are even goats."

Gran chuckled. "Oh, dear."

"He's in love."

"And this is Judd Harlow's place? The pilot who flew you to Chicago?"

Savannah played with the hem of her tank top. *The pilot, the sexy bear of a man, the hero who'd taken them under his wing when they'd needed it most…*

"Yup," she said, hoping Gran couldn't read the look on her face. The one that said she was more taken with Judd than she was comfortable with.

But there was no use. Gran noticed everything.

Her soft blue gaze settled on Savannah's. "He's a good man," she said. "I've heard the Harlow boys are all good men."

"They are," Savannah said.

But instead of digging like Savannah fully expected her to, Gran smiled and sat back in her chair, her head shaking gently back and forth. "Every good man needs a good woman," she said matter-of-factly. And then, "I'm getting hungry, pumpkin. How about you?"

Chapter Eight

SAVANNAH TURNED DOWN the old country lane at a quarter to six. The sun was low in the sky, setting the wispy clouds on fire. The scenery had been beautiful this afternoon, but in the golden light of early evening, it was breathtaking.

The white house in the distance was plain but lovely, holding court in the middle of the farm like a proper lady. But it was the barn, red and peeling from decades of exposure to the harsh Montana elements, that really stole her heart. Its roof was sagging, but had been lovingly repaired throughout the years—a patchwork of colors where the shingles didn't match, or boards had been placed to fix weak spots. The pasture fences surrounded it, hugging it with elderly arms.

Tall grass swayed in the breeze and lazy bugs flitted in the air, reminding her of country stars. The smell of hay drifted through the cracked windows of her car, and she almost sneezed, realizing she hadn't smelled hay, honest-to-goodness *hay*, since she was little.

She came to a stop in front of the yard where the kids were playing. Wyatt grinned and waved, but went right back to what he was doing with Maddie. Something that involved a paper airplane.

Turning the engine off, she looked over to see Judd heading down the porch steps, his strides long and purposeful, as usual.

She reached over and grabbed the package from the passenger's seat. She hadn't had time to wrap it very well—she'd just used tissue paper and a plain blue ribbon, but it fit somehow. Like the house itself, and the barn that reveled in its uncomplicated beauty.

"Hey," he said, as she opened the door and stepped into the evening air. "How was your day?"

She watched him for a second, taken off guard by the question, by the tone of it. But he did that. Had a way of making her feel like the answer was important to him.

He put his hands in his pockets and looked down at her, his eyes unreadable. He wore another western shirt today, this one blue plaid, with the sleeves rolled up to his elbows. There was scruff on his jaw, and evidence of sun on his face. If she didn't know better, she'd think he'd been born and raised on this farm. He fit here, like a piece to an old, forgotten puzzle.

"I should've told you to drop Wyatt off a few hours earlier so you could have a little time to yourself," he continued. "I know you probably don't get a ton of that." He shrugged, as if this was something he offered every mom in town, and he'd just forgotten his manners.

Savannah had to work not to stare at him. But a distinctive warmth unfurled inside her chest as she stood there, the breeze moving through her loose hair.

She tucked her long bangs behind one ear. "That's so sweet of you. But I had enough time to go see my gran. Sometimes it's hard to get to talk with Wyatt there, so that was a treat. Thank you."

Nodding, he glanced toward the kids in the yard. "They're still playing. Had a good time, I think he likes it out here."

"Who wouldn't?"

He looked down at the package in her hands.

"Oh," she said, holding it out. "I almost forgot. I made this for you."

Raising his brows, he took it.

"Well, for your house. It's a housewarming present."

"You didn't have to do that," he said. "But thank you. Should I open it now?"

She grinned, unable to help it, and nodded.

He unwrapped the paper, his big fingers surprisingly nimble. He barely tore it, and she wondered if he was an obsessive recycler like she was.

He stared down at the spiral glass sphere in his hand, and held it up, the wind immediately making it spin. It was Coca-Cola–red, the same red as the barn behind them. The glass caught the light of the setting sun, and the frozen air bubbles suspended inside looked like lava.

"It's a wind spinner," she said. "To hang on your porch."

"You made this?"

She nodded. "I work out of a little studio in town. I get over there as much as I can, but it's hard to leave Wyatt, so…" She chewed the inside of her cheek for a second, before adding softly, "Someday I want my own studio."

Her heart thumped as she realized she'd never told anyone that before. It sounded too far-fetched, even to her own ears, and she was protective of her dreams. But Judd was different. She'd sensed that from the beginning.

He wrapped the spinner gently back in the paper. "I know exactly where I'm going to hang it. Thank you."

She smiled. She could tell he liked it, and that made her happy.

"Look," he said. "You want a little tour? The kids are having fun, we have some daylight left."

She was hoping he'd offer. She'd always wanted to see inside the Tucker house.

"I'd love that," she said.

And she followed him toward the porch steps, trying not to look at his butt the entire way.

JUDD WISHED MORE of his boxes were unpacked. But at least the furniture was out, and his stuff looked surprisingly good inside the old place. He'd always favored simple lines, uncomplicated colors and textures, and that complimented the house. Still, he couldn't help but wonder how a woman's touch might make it come alive. Transform it from a house to a home.

They walked now toward the barn, the kids' distant laughter echoing through the evening air.

Judd reached up and pulled the barn door back on its track. It rumbled and squeaked, but moved easily enough over the rollers. They were met with the immediate smell of straw, and of animals that had long since moved on. Their scent lingered—a certain farmy perfume that either you loved, or you hated. There was no in-between.

Savannah apparently loved it. She closed her eyes, tilted her head back, and breathed deep, her breasts rising underneath her gray hoodie.

She was beautiful, and Judd had the sudden urge to kiss her. Not just kiss her, but push her up against one of the old stall doors and move his hand under that hoodie. He wanted to feel her skin against his palm and hear her voice in his ear.

Looking away out of pure necessity, he reached up to tug a chain connected to a single light bulb.

"Here it is," he said. "It needs cleaning up, but it's a great place for the plane."

The 1956 Cessna Skyhawk sat like a rusted-out beauty in the corner of the barn, her wings reaching for them in angelic optimism.

Savannah stared at it, her mouth hanging open. "Oh, my God. It's gorgeous."

He knew better. It was broken down, maybe beyond anything he could do for it, but it was the plane of his dreams. The one that had set his boyhood aviation dreams on fire. He remembered the first picture of a Skyhawk he'd seen in a magazine, and he'd never been the same since.

"I don't know about beautiful...maybe once. I'm hoping she will be again. It was a great deal, though. I've been looking for one I could afford for years. This one just fell into my lap and I couldn't say no."

Savannah walked over to the plane, and reached a tentative hand up to touch its wing. He thought of himself as pretty jaded when it all came down to it, but was surprised to find his heart beating heavier than normal inside his chest. As he watched her look up at the Skyhawk in such wonder, it reminded him of why he loved flying so much. Always had.

But Savannah hated flying, which made this moment infinitely more interesting. Maybe it was the soft evening light pouring in through the slats of the barn. Maybe it was the contradiction of that lighting against the plane's old paint job, that should be homely all these years later, but absolutely wasn't. Whatever it was, it seemed the Skyhawk's rock-and-roll charm wasn't just reserved for him. Savannah felt it, too. And that moved him.

"The lines of it," she said. "It makes me think of celebrities in the 50s and 60s." She turned. "I can almost see them in their hats and suits climbing in."

"You must've read the same magazines I did."

"Or watched the same movies. What was the one about Ritchie Valens? *La Bamba?*"

"Oh, Jesus. No, that was a Beechcraft Bonanza. And hopefully this one won't have the same kind of fate."

"Never," she said, running her fingers over the wing, leaving trails in the grainy dust.

He came up behind her. "It'll be a while until I get it in the air. There's a lot to fix."

She was still looking up at the plane and he let his gaze

drop to her hair. He could smell it from where he stood—
the shampoo she'd used that morning. He wanted to touch
it. Even more, wrap the silky, mink-colored strands in his
fist.

Without thinking, he reached over her and ran his hand
along the wing where she'd left her fingerprints. She stepped
back and bumped into him, her ass soft and giving against
his groin.

"Oh…" Her cheeks flushed pink. "Sorry."

He wasn't sorry. At all. But since he considered himself a
gentleman, he stepped away to give her room to walk
around. She continued inspecting the Skyhawk as though
she was ready to put an offer down, but kept glancing over
and catching his eye as a charged silence settled between
them.

"I can't tell you how much I appreciate you flying Wyatt
and me to Chicago," she finally said, clasping her hands
together.

"You know I'm happy to do it."

"Only two weeks. It feels like we've been waiting forever,
and now it's finally here. I can't believe it."

Judd was glad he took these six weeks off. The timing
was perfect. But he would've adjusted his schedule to make it
happen anyway.

"Is he nervous?" he asked.

"Nope. Not yet. He's so excited to be flying with you
again that I'm not even sure the surgery part has registered
yet."

Judd smiled. "He's a good kid. Fearless."

"I know. That's what worries me. I've spent so long protecting him, I'm not going to know what to do with myself when he gets old enough to venture out on his own."

"You're a great mom. You'll figure it out."

She smiled back. "Thank you. I try. I think the hardest part of raising him on my own is not having anyone to bounce things off of. Like, sometimes I have no idea if what I'm doing is right. I just have to hope it's close and move on."

Judd leaned against the plane and crossed his arms over his chest. Savannah stood by the tail, her hands still clasped. Every now and then she'd rock forward on the toes of her tennis shoes, then back down again. She was giving him the distinct impression of being nervous. Which only made him want to do things to make her *un*-nervous.

He watched her, thinking of the barbeque the other day, and the call she'd taken from her ex-husband. Normally he'd keep his mouth shut, but what she'd just said hit a nerve. She was neck deep in the task of raising a little boy on her own. He couldn't stand the thought of that prick talking his way back in after what he'd done. Again, he thought of his own mother, and what she'd had to accomplish on her own, too. Only she'd always let the creeps back in. *Always.*

Judd had said before he wasn't good at beating around the bush. And he wasn't. He settled his gaze directly on hers. "I know he called the other day. Your ex. Is he gonna help after the surgery?"

Savannah's shoulders stiffened. Maybe it was the fact that he'd asked. Or maybe it was the mention of her ex-husband that she had an aversion to. Regardless, the light around her seemed to dim a little.

After another few seconds, she sighed. "I don't know. He says he wants to come visit… It's a long story."

"I've got time. If you feel like telling it."

She put her hands in her pockets. "I know what you're thinking. I shouldn't let him anywhere near Wyatt."

"It's none of my business."

"But you're probably thinking it."

"I think a lot of things. I've got my own experiences to draw from, but they're not yours. No matter how I feel, I haven't walked in your shoes."

She nodded. "I have to be honest…I haven't talked to many people about this. Mary and my gran. That's about it. But it feels good to be asked. I'm just afraid…"

"Of what?"

"Of being judged, I guess. Of saying the wrong thing. Of saying too much."

Judd stepped toward her. The sun had finally disappeared behind the mountains in the west, and the light was changing fast. He could still hear the kids playing near the house, but they'd need to come in soon.

It seemed like every time he saw Savannah Casteele, he ended up wanting more. More time, more conversation, more *her*. He thought about inviting her and Wyatt to stay for dinner, but quickly dismissed it. If he wasn't careful, he'd end up having to explain why he'd led her on, or why he wasn't ready for any kind of relationship.

Even so, he hated the thought of her leaving tonight.

Hated the thought of the distant laughter in the yard dying away. So he did the only thing he could think of to keep her there longer, and took another step closer.

She stared up at him, the pulse in her neck visible from where he stood. There were a few tiny freckles scattered across her nose. They only made her lovelier in that moment where late afternoon gave way to dusk, and fat bullfrogs croaked from the pond near the road.

She was waiting for him to make some kind of move. To say something, *do* something. Right now, for whatever damn reason, she trusted him to lead the way. And he felt it all the way to his core.

He hadn't been planning on touching her. He'd only meant to tell her that he'd listen if she ever needed to talk. That he'd be a friend if she needed one. But her eyes were so green, they reminded him of Marietta River in the summertime. Her chest rose and fell with nerves, and he couldn't have helped himself if he'd tried.

He bent his head slightly. Her full lips were parted—maybe anticipating something that he was more than willing to give.

Their gazes locked, and it seemed that time had decided to hold up and wait on them. To see what it was they were going to do with this quiet opportunity.

And then Judd came the rest of the way. Bending, he kissed her so gently, he could feel her lips quiver underneath his. A sound escaped her throat—something soft and feminine, and vaguely hungry. It only made his heart knock harder in his chest, but he fought the instinct to pull her closer. He was half expecting her to push him away, and God help him, he didn't know if he could take that.

So he took all the pleasure he could get in the taste of her, the feel of her, the scent of her. He didn't urge her lips open with his tongue like he wanted to. Instead, he lingered on her mouth for a few more delicious seconds, before forcing himself to break the kiss.

He pulled away and looked down at her. Her eyes had been closed, and they opened again to settle on him with dreamy awareness. Some of the nerves were gone. He'd managed to kiss those away. But in their place was something else that set his veins on fire. He wondered how long it had been since she'd been with a man. From the look on her face, probably a while, and he railed against the sudden ridiculous need to offer her anything she wanted in bed. Anything at all.

He rubbed the back of his neck. "Would you believe I was just going to offer an ear to bend?"

A smile crept across her lips. "I think I might believe anything you said right now."

There was an undercurrent crackling between them. Keeping his hands off her was proving to be one of the hardest things he'd ever done.

"Judd," she said. "I want to—"

She was cut off by the sound of footsteps in the gravel outside.

"Mama!" Wyatt yelled. "Come see Darryl's trick! Maddie taught him!"

They stared at each other.

"Another night," Judd said, his voice low.

And realized that could mean a lot of things.

Chapter Nine

SAVANNAH WALKED TOWARD the hangar with Wyatt firmly holding her hand. They were early. She was always early when she was nervous, and today she was shaking in her boots. Literally.

The warm spring weather Montana had grown unwisely accustomed to these past few weeks, had given way to its usual blustery cold, and she tugged at the collar of her coat as if a few more inches of downy warmth would suddenly materialize.

Wyatt looked up, his cheeks red. "Is he inside, Mama?"

Something that had also happened in the past few weeks was Wyatt's ever-growing idolization of Judd Harlow. Savannah couldn't decide how to feel about it. On one hand, she could understand. She was also starting to idolize Judd, which was dangerous and stupid, and didn't make any sense whatsoever to her single-mother heart. Yes, he'd kissed her. And yes, he'd been incredibly kind to them both, going out of his way to make her life just a little easier.

But that made her wary of him, too. Because that kindness felt good. And as easily as he'd offered it up, he could snatch it away again. And then where would she be? In another position of having to explain to her little boy where his idol went. That scared her to death. She'd been so scared in fact, that after Judd had kissed her that night in the barn, she'd been careful not to be alone with him. She wasn't in any position to be broken again. Or even bruised up again. Right now she had to focus on this surgery, on how to handle the possibility of Steven being more involved in their lives, of making a decent enough living to support her little family on her own. She couldn't fall in love right now, or even fall in lust. She didn't have that luxury.

And still, she sensed in Judd an admiration in just that. He hadn't had a mother who'd put him first, or who'd thought of the repercussions of her actions at all. So even as Savannah pushed him away to protect her son, she also felt that was one of the things he was drawn to about her. It was a catch twenty-two.

The door to the hangar opened. When Wyatt saw Judd standing there, he yanked his hand from Savannah's and ran like a puppy into his arms.

Catching him, Judd lifted him over his head, bouncing him a couple of times for good measure, then settled him against his hip.

"Hey, buddy. You all set?"

Savannah's heart squeezed. She felt like she did a pretty good job of giving Wyatt what he needed in the form of love and affection. But there was no denying he longed for a man in his life.

Wyatt grinned from ear to ear, making his lip soften. Pretty soon, there'd only be a scar left. And even that would fade over time.

"All set!" he said.

Judd looked over at Savannah. "How about you, Mom?"

She stepped closer, pulling her suitcase behind her. It rolled hollowly over the concrete. "Ready as I'll ever be." She frowned, noticing the shadows underneath Judd's eyes. The fact that he hadn't shaved, which was incredibly sexy, but wasn't jiving with the meticulous pilot persona he'd exuded last time she'd gotten on his plane.

"Are you okay?" she asked.

"Fine. Just wanted to get here early to watch some weather that's come up."

"Oh, God."

"Nothing to worry about," he said. "You trust me, right?"

Swallowing, she nodded.

"Just making sure, that's all."

She wanted to go to him. To hug him for all this. And maybe she wanted to kiss him, too, and finish what they'd started two weeks ago. But that went directly against all the self-coaching she'd done lately. She'd maintain a healthy distance. No less, no more. No matter how blue his eyes were, or how handsome he looked this early in the morning. *A healthy distance...*

Judd put Wyatt gently on the ground. "Plane's open, buddy. Why don't you hop in and we'll be right there. Need to get going in a few."

"Okay!"

Wyatt didn't need to be told twice. He ran over to the

Cessna with his backpack bouncing, and climbed up the steps.

He disappeared from view, leaving Savannah with nothing to do but gaze up at the man in front of her. Despite all the lectures she'd given herself, despite all the stern warnings, she couldn't help but be swayed by that gorgeous face. By the way he smelled, like a hockey player fresh out of the locker room.

Her belly tightened as a sudden gust of wind buffeted the hangar, making the aluminum siding knock against itself.

He stared down at her, and for a second, she thought he might kiss her again. All those stupid lectures flew right out the window as she found herself hoping he would. She squeezed the suitcase handle and waited.

"Don't worry," he said.

"Don't worry…" she repeated lamely. "About?"

Was this going to be the part where he brought up what happened in the barn? And if so, what would she say? That she regretted it? Because that wouldn't be true. It worried her, yes. And they probably shouldn't do it again. But she didn't regret it, not for a second. In fact, she'd relived that moment over and over again, memorizing every detail— every sound, every touch, every image.

"About the weather," he said evenly.

"Oh…"

"What'd you think I meant?"

Shrugging, she looked away, embarrassed. Maybe he kissed all his female visitors in his charming old barn, for all she knew. Maybe she didn't have to worry about him trying to kiss her again, because maybe she wasn't anything special.

"Savannah?" He reached out and put his fingertips underneath her chin, guiding her back to face him. Such a simple gesture, but a very, very masculine one. "Are you ever going to talk to me, or are you gonna keep shutting down like this?"

"I don't shut down."

"That's all you've been doing. I haven't wanted to push, but at some point we need to acknowledge what happened the other night."

So, there it was. Despite everything, she felt a sweet rush of relief. That meant it had meant something to him, too.

"I'm sorry," she said. "It caught me off guard, that's all."

He nodded.

"It's just that Wyatt has to be my first priority right now."

"I get that about you."

"As much as I'm attracted…as much as I want you to…"

Crossing his arms over his chest, he gazed down at her.

She squirmed under that gaze, wondering how it was that one man could make her so tongue-tied.

Taking a deep breath, she rubbed her thumb over the handle of the suitcase, and looked past Judd's giant shoulder to her son in the Cessna. His nose was pressed up against the window.

Honesty's always the best policy… Gran had taught her that.

She looked back at Judd, and tried not to be undone by him. By everything he represented. And instead, she focused on what she knew in her heart to be the smartest thing.

"I can't let myself fall for anyone right now," she said matter-of-factly. "No matter how much I loved that kiss...and I did love that kiss..." Her face heated. "I have to be there for Wyatt. Not just some of me. All of me."

Judd slowly put his hands in his pockets. "I'm not asking you to *marry* me, Savannah."

The words stung, even though he probably hadn't meant for them to. No, he definitely wasn't asking that.

"I think you're making this harder than it has to be," he continued.

She forced her shoulders back, not wanting him to see how much he'd hurt her feelings. "Maybe it's easy for you to go around kissing people, but it's different for me."

There were so many other things she could say—*I haven't been with anyone for a really long time... No guy's ever been this nice to me... I'm scared you'll break my heart...* But they were all so humiliating, she bit them back before they could escape. Thank God.

Instead, she stared up at him, defiance masking the hurt.

"You make it sound like that's a habit of mine," he said. "Kissing people."

"Maybe it is. How would I know?"

"You wouldn't. You'd just have to trust me. But you don't trust many people, do you?"

She didn't answer that.

"It doesn't have to be hard, Savannah. It could just be fun."

Fun... She didn't call getting her heart pulverized fun.

Which was exactly what was going to happen if he kept looking at her like that.

"So you're the one-night stand type?" she said. "Is that it?"

She'd meant for it to be biting, but he smiled devilishly. "Get your mind out of the gutter."

"What else would you call it?"

"I never mentioned sex. But I wouldn't deny you if that's what you want."

She laughed, unable to help it. He was ridiculous. And turning her on, in spite of everything.

"Are you going to fly us to Chicago, or not?"

"Maybe. If you consider kissing me again."

"Judd…"

His smile faded, and she immediately wanted it back in all its electric vitality. She was apparently going to be a huge walking contradiction where he was concerned. She wanted him, but she wanted him at an arm's length. She knew she couldn't keep this up for long. Something was going to have to give.

"I'd fly you to Chicago even if you swore me off forever," he said, his voice low. "But I hope you won't."

She watched him. The reality was, he wasn't her knight in shining armor. He was just a really, really nice guy, who also happened to be sexier than anyone she'd ever met. He wasn't going to go sweeping her off her feet and settle down with a ready-made family. That wasn't how life worked. At least not any kind of life she'd ever known.

Without waiting for an answer, Judd reached around and

grabbed her suitcase. Even though it was as big as she was, he lifted it like it weighed nothing at all. He turned toward the Cessna and walked away, giving her an unobstructed view of his broad, sexy back.

She sighed heavily. As long as she was thinking reality, she knew she'd probably kiss him again…

He turned and eyed her over his shoulder. "You coming?"

Yup. Definitely kissing him again.

SAVANNAH SAT IN the chair next to Wyatt's bed. He was in his gown, and the IV had been placed a few minutes ago. They hadn't been able to find a vein right away, and he'd cried and struggled toward the end, which had been almost more than she could take.

But overall, he'd been an absolute trouper since they'd walked through the door, and at the moment, he seemed relatively at ease—playing with his Nintendo, and looking up at the muted TV every now and then.

It was Savannah who was anxious. Up until today, she'd been so overcome with relief that she could pay for the surgery, the idea of needing some kind of support during the actual event hadn't occurred to her. Mary had offered to come, but at the time Savannah had felt it might be easier if she handled it alone. Now, she wasn't so sure.

She reached out and smoothed her son's hair, smiling when he touched her hand.

"Love you, Mama."

"I love you, too, baby."

"When do we get to go home?"

"Only a few days. Judd will come pick us up, and then you'll get to watch cartoons on the couch and have all the ice cream you want, okay?"

He nodded. "Will Maddie come see me?"

"I bet wild horses wouldn't keep her away."

"And Granny?"

Savannah's heart swelled. "Yup."

"And Auntie Mary?"

"And Auntie Mary, too." He was listing the most important people in his orbit. And it was very small. Another reminder of how crucial she was to him—she was really all he had.

There was a soft knock on the door, and Doctor Lieu walked in.

She was petite and attractive, her silky black hair pulled back into a neat bun. She wore black horn-rimmed glasses, and looked every bit the brilliant surgeon.

Smiling at Wyatt, she patted his knee.

"How's it going in here?" she asked, her voice light and airy. She sounded like a Disney princess. "I heard there was a brave boy in this room, so I had to come see him with my very own eyeballs." She squinted, making him giggle.

She turned to Savannah. "How are you doing, Ms. Casteele?"

"Pretty well. We're just ready to get this over with."

"I know you are. It's going to go very smoothly, very

quickly, okay?"

Savannah nodded, suddenly so overcome with emotion that she had to look away.

Doctor Lieu noticed, and touched her shoulder. "It's a lot," she said quietly, so Wyatt wouldn't hear. "Honestly, it's going to be harder on you than it will be on him. My advice would be to grab something to eat, take a walk around the hospital. Do something other than sit in the waiting room, if you can. We'll get in touch right away if we need you. Try and take care of yourself, too, okay?"

Savannah smiled, not trusting herself to speak. Doctor Lieu was right, of course. She didn't want to fall apart now, after all the appointments, second opinions, months of saving, and getting emotionally prepared. It was a wonderful day. So she didn't know why it was all hitting like this. So hard, so abrupt.

Taking an even breath, she looked over at Wyatt. They'd given him a sedative and he rubbed his eyes, looking sleepy. Bless his little heart. He was the best thing that had ever happened to her. And again, she found herself in the strange place of being thankful for Steven, despite all the pain he'd inflicted over the years. She needed to learn to forgive him. Maybe then they could coexist lovingly, if that was possible.

Doctor Lieu looked at the chart in her hand and spoke softly to a nurse who'd just come in.

"Okay, Mom we're ready to go. You can walk him to the double doors outside. I promise we'll take excellent care of him."

"I know you will. Thank you."

She looked down at Wyatt who looked back with a frown. His first since getting his IV.

"Mama…don't go. Please, Mommy."

"Oh, honey." She brushed his hair back from his forehead and kissed it. "You're so brave. I'll be right here when you wake up, okay?"

He nodded, but his eyes filled with tears. They spilled over his cheeks and dripped off his trembling chin. But he didn't make a sound.

Savannah had to bite her lip to keep from crying herself. Fighting for even breaths, she watched as the nurses pulled the bars up on the bed and kicked the stoppers away from its wheels.

Wyatt gripped her fingers as they wheeled him into the hallway. Orderlies in colorful scrubs walked past, doctors were being paged overhead, somewhere down the hall, someone was crying.

Still, she and Wyatt held on to each other. Walking beside the bed, she nodded politely at the small talk one of the nurses tried to make, but she only had eyes and ears for Wyatt. Her maternal instincts were in overdrive as she struggled to read his expression, to feel if his hand was shaking.

The nurses slowed and gave her a sympathetic look. Their eyes were kind, but she could see in them a quiet resolve. They were seasoned veterans, saw this kind of thing on a daily basis. Watched families struggle, and sometimes overcome. Sometimes not… Their stoic expressions gave Savannah the strength she needed to lean down and kiss her little boy on the cheek, and pry his fingers loose from hers. Even though she thought a layer of her heart would come with them.

"I love you so much," she whispered next to his temple. He smelled like his surroundings, like starched hospital gown and sheets. But he also smelled familiar, like baby shampoo. "Be my big, brave boy, okay? I'll see you soon."

And then they were wheeling him through the doors, his sobs breaking her in two.

Only when the doors closed behind him, did she allow herself to lean against the wall and cry.

Chapter Ten

JUDD WATCHED THE Chicago landscape rush past his window in a blur of concrete and brake lights. The cab was stuffy and smelled like stale cigarettes. He was tired and irritable. There were a shit-ton of boxes to unpack at the house, which he wasn't looking forward to. But he *was* looking forward to his own bed and being back at the farm again, which meant spending more time with Maddie. Working on the plane, feeding the damn goats which he was becoming inconveniently attached to. Farm life turned out to be everything he never knew he'd always wanted.

Rubbing the back of his neck, he closed his eyes for a second. There was staticky music playing over the radio, something country and vaguely familiar. It reminded him of home.

"In town for business or pleasure?" the cabbie asked, chewing on a toothpick and eyeing him in the rearview mirror.

Frowning, Judd looked at the older man's reflection. "Neither," he said. "A friend's son is having surgery. Just made sure they got checked into the hospital okay."

Calling Savannah a friend didn't quite fit. He guessed

she was. Technically. But also technically, he wanted to remove her underwear with his teeth. So, there was that.

The cabbie nodded, moving the toothpick to the other side of his mouth. "What kind of surgery?"

"Cleft lip."

"Oooh. That's a tough one, isn't it?"

No matter how much time Judd spent flying in and out of new cities he never got used to how forward people could be. In Marietta, a man's business was his own. Not that folks didn't discuss it when his back was turned, but still. The way things worked in Montana had always suited Judd, since he'd never been a big talker, and definitely wasn't a fan of oversharing.

"It is," he said, looking out the window. "It's a tough one."

"Poor kid. That's a rough break."

He thought about Wyatt, picturing the way he'd looked leaning against his mother as they descended toward the city. She'd cradled him as he'd slept, patting his leg every now and then as if needing to comfort him. Or herself.

She'd impressed Judd on the flight though, turning white as a sheet during takeoff, but weathering the significant turbulence like a pro. He'd looked at her and she stared wide-eyed back, never saying a word, knowing Wyatt was watching her closely.

The cabbie took the exit toward the airport, and Judd's chest tightened. He looked down at his watch. Wyatt should be in surgery by now. He'd gotten a text from Savannah about an hour ago.

IV is in, thank God! Just waiting for them to take him back. Thank you again for everything! See you in a few days.

The cabbie turned the radio to an oldies station, and something from the 70s crackled out. He was talking about the weather now, and how he was pretty sure this summer would shape up to be a hell of a lot hotter than last summer, and how were the summers where Judd was from?

Judd could only nod in response, because he wasn't thinking about the weather, or summer, or even home anymore. He was thinking about Savannah sitting in that waiting room alone. With nobody to bring her coffee, or wrap an arm around her, or to tell her it was going to be okay. She was by herself in a strange city, while her kid was having a pretty significant surgery.

Clenching his jaw, he ran a hand through his hair.

"Someday me and the missus are gonna retire somewhere on the beach," the cabbie said, rubbing his thumbs along the steering wheel. "Somewhere tropical. Just have to pad that nest egg a little more. Only the best for my old lady, you know?"

Judd watched the cabbie's reflection in the rearview mirror—the faded blue eyes, the unshaven chin, the brown hair threaded with gray. The guy was rough around the edges, yeah. But he obviously had a good heart. He loved his wife. And again, Judd pictured Savannah for a reason he didn't entirely understand.

He leaned forward. "Hey, man…"

The cabbie glanced back.

"Can you turn around?" Judd asked.

"Turn around…and go back the way we came?"

"Yeah."

"To the hospital?"

"Please."

The cabbie smiled. "Ahh. Your lady friend?"

"How'd you know she was a lady?"

"Because it's written all over your face, son. The farther we got from that hospital, the quieter you got. Don't want to leave her just yet, do you?"

Judd sat back against the seat wondering what he was getting himself into.

But knowing if people could see it written on his damn face, he was in some serious trouble.

>>><<<

SAVANNAH STOOD LOOKING out the waiting room window to the city below. She'd taken Doctor Lieu's advice and had gone for a walk, managing to choke down a vending machine granola bar along the way.

But in the end, she hadn't been able to go far. She'd ended up right back where she'd started, pacing and glancing up at the clock every five minutes.

There was a large, uncomfortable lump in her throat that seemed to have taken up residence there. She'd cried earlier, but it had done nothing to dislodge it. Staring out the window, she'd finally accepted that this surgery was a really big deal. And as a single parent, she was just going to have to shoulder things like this the best way she knew how.

Taking a deep breath, she promised herself she'd talk to Mary when she got home. She'd try and lean on her best friend like she knew Mary wanted to be leaned on. It was okay to need some help. But Savannah always had trouble asking, no matter how difficult the circumstances.

She took a sip of the lukewarm coffee in her hand and stared down at the tiny little Monopoly cars below.

"I was worried I wouldn't get back in time."

Savannah startled. *Judd?* She turned to see him standing behind her. Hands in his pockets, plaid shirt open at the throat. A sight for sore, sore eyes.

She smiled, her ears on fire. Her breasts on fire. Every single bit of her on fire, while her heart beat like something out of a middle school band.

"You came back," she said.

"I never should've left."

"You've already done so much for us, Judd. Don't you have to get back to Marietta?"

His gaze settled on hers, but not before dropping to take in her body. She wore jeans and a pale pink blouse—nothing special, but he had this way of looking at her, though…

"I don't have to get back right away," he said. "How are you doing? Okay?"

The question stroked her insides like a warm hand easing a sore spot.

"I'm…I'm…" And then her voice caught. Like it had been wanting to all morning—any time the nurses had looked in her direction, or Doctor Lieu smiled at her, or when she'd asked one of the janitors where the bathroom was. She thought she'd cried all her tears when they'd wheeled Wyatt away, but she was wrong.

She felt her face crumple, and for a second, there was the sharp embarrassment of losing her composure in front of someone. And not just anyone. In front of Judd.

But before her cheeks could even heat properly, he'd gathered her into his arms.

His chest was broad and solid. His shirt smelled fresh and clean, and was soft against her skin. He was warm—really warm. And the arms that encircled her were so powerful that she felt completely cut off from the rest of the world. From pain and uncertainty, and the questions that had dogged her all morning. For the past four years, if she was being honest. *Am I a good mother? What if something happens to me? Will I be able to give him what he needs? Will I raise a man who will choose to stay when things get tough, or will he run like his dad?*

She cried, trying to be quiet about it, but it was like some kind of cathartic release that she'd needed more than she'd known. Slowly, slowly, those doubts and fears receded like a wave from a beach, leaving her soaked, but still breathing.

His heart beat strong and sure against her cheek and she realized she'd made a wet spot on his shirt.

Wiping her eyes, she pulled away enough to laugh. "I'm sorry. I don't even know where that came from."

He stared down at her, looking worried. Like she might shatter right in front of him.

He caught a stray tear with the backs of his knuckles. "Don't be ridiculous. You're under a lot of stress, Savannah."

Everything about Judd Harlow seemed to dwarf her in that moment—his size, his words, his essence. She felt herself falling, even as she imagined reaching for something solid to grab on to.

"I..." she began, but then realized she didn't know what to say.

He didn't seem to hear her anyway. Slowly, he bent his head toward hers. His gaze held her captive, pinned there like something small and helpless. Only she wasn't helpless. She could stop him anytime. But she didn't want to. She wanted him to come the rest of the way. Every inch of the way until he was not only touching her, but was *inside* her.

The thought born of pure, raw desire, made her flesh burn.

His breath puffed warm against her lips. He smelled like mint. Her belly coiled, anticipating the feel of his stubble scraping her chin. Her nipples tingled underneath her sensible, cotton bra.

And then he kissed her. It was different from the kiss in the barn. It should've been less intense, because they weren't exactly alone in the hospital. But somehow, that only made it hotter—the sheer nakedness of it all.

He wrapped a muscular arm around her lower back and pulled her close. She could feel the hard contours of his belt buckle against her stomach. His thighs were thick and rigid against her own. His tongue nudged at her lips and she opened her mouth without any convincing on his part. He slipped inside, wet and skillful, and the taste of him nearly made her knees buckle.

He must've felt her sway, because his arm tightened around her waist.

Even though he was the strong one, she felt him yielding to her, too. She felt his heart pound, his skin heat. *She* was doing this to him. She, who'd never felt particularly powerful at anything, except when she was standing in front of a fire, making glass bend to her will.

That's what it felt like now. This stolen kiss in the cold, lonely waiting room. She felt Judd bending to her will. She thought if they weren't in this hospital right now, he might even be begging for something she wasn't sure she knew how to give yet. Her body? Her heart? It was all moving so fast.

Slowly, he broke the kiss.

Her eyes had been closed…for how long? It felt like a lifetime, but had probably only been a moment or two. She opened them, realizing she'd almost forgotten her son was in surgery.

She looked guiltily up at the clock and touched her lips which were wet and tingling.

His gaze followed hers. "How long now?"

"He should be out soon. I can't believe it's almost over…the waiting."

"I know it's been a long morning."

"Long morning…long four years."

He frowned.

"I don't mean that the way it sounds," she said quickly. "Having Wyatt was the biggest blessing. I meant his lip, Steven taking off. My gran having to move out of her house… It's just been hard."

87

"I know it has. And as far as Steven goes…" He paused, looking like he wanted to say the right thing. "I know what you said before. But do you think there's a possibility he *could've* left because of Wyatt's lip?"

It was a bold question. Bold because it didn't leave Steven a whole lot of benefit of the doubt. As far as she was concerned, anyone who'd abandon their child because of a physical deformity wasn't worth their bus ticket out of town. But she had to admit, there were times when she'd wondered the same thing about her ex-husband.

She'd finally come to realize the answers were never going to be cut-and-dried where Steven was concerned. He had issues that stretched out long before they'd gotten married, before Wyatt had come along.

She shook her head. "I don't think so. He struggled with it, and I could never forgive him for that. But he left because he wasn't ready to be a father. Or to be married. He left because he was too young and had a crapload of growing up to do."

The muscles in Judd's jaw bunched. "You were young too, and you didn't abandon your kid."

"No, I didn't."

"Seems like you might be going a little easy on the guy."

She wrapped her arms around her waist, suddenly cold. "I try to be diplomatic about Steven. He's Wyatt's dad and he had a rough childhood…"

Judd didn't say anything. She could tell he was trying not to overstep.

"You think I let people walk on me," she said. "Don't

you?"

"What? No."

"Come on. I can tell. The naive mom who can't tell her ex-husband to go to hell where he belongs, right?"

Slowly, his skin flushed red. She'd hit a nerve. That had been a dumb thing to say. She could've been describing his own mother.

"I think you're anything but naive," he finally said, his voice low. "But I wouldn't mind if you told him to go to hell."

"It's not that easy."

He shrugged. Again, she could see he was biting his tongue. She was tired of people tiptoeing around the subject of Steven because they were afraid they'd say the wrong thing. Yes, it was painful, but she wasn't a china doll, either. She could talk about it just fine. In fact, there was a part of her that longed to talk about it, if only to gain a different perspective.

They were standing by the waiting room coffeepot, and an elderly gentleman reached apologetically around her for a Styrofoam cup. She smiled at him before looking back up at Judd. "Say what you think. I want to hear it."

"You probably don't."

"I appreciate you not wanting to offend me," she said evenly. "But I think we're kind of past that point, don't you think? You just had your tongue in my mouth."

He raised his brows.

"Yeah," she said. "That's right. So just talk to me. This is what people do. This is what *friends* do, if you want to call us that. They talk to each other. They give advice, they open up. I've been the only one sharing anything so far. It's your turn."

He put his hands in his pockets. "I don't know what you want me to say. I'm never gonna be the type of guy who's going to forgive a man who walks out on his family."

"Okay...and?"

"*And* my mother did that. She was constantly being shit on, and she was constantly forgiving for the sake of forgetting."

"You think I'd do the same?"

"I told you. It's none of my business."

That hurt. Like stepping on a rock with her bare feet. Technically, it wasn't his business. But shouldn't he care about this part of her life by now, even a little? Enough to talk about it with her for God's sake?

She was beginning to see how stubborn he really was. And that he was probably used to women moving delicately around that part of his personality in order to reap the benefits of his other assets. But she wasn't in the mood for those right now. She wanted to go deeper.

"I'm calling bullshit," she said.

"Really."

"Yes," she said. "Because I can tell you have more to say. And this is me telling you that I care about what you have to say, how you feel."

He watched her steadily, the pulse tapping at the base of his neck. She understood this was a defining moment. He would have to make a decision—back away from something that made him uncomfortable. Or lean into it and see where it might take him. The former was safe. The latter was a risk, and one that could have implications for them both.

And then, surprising her, he leaned close.

"You want me to say how I really feel?"

She nodded, her mouth dry.

"Okay, then…"

The waiting room had gone still. Her heart thudded in her ears.

"I feel like you're too good for that asshole," he said, his voice barely above a whisper now. "It makes me see fucking red that he'd want to come back after all this time. And, yeah. I get growing up and experiencing come-to-Jesus moments, and all that shit people do when they mature, but I don't get, for one goddamn minute, leaving that little boy in there. And you. Leaving you. It's beyond my capability. So, if you want me to be a good guy and support you no matter what, I will. Because I care about you. But if you want my opinion, you'd better be careful asking for it. Because sugarcoating shit is not my specialty."

She stared up at him. She'd poked a bear, and he'd woken up. His words, the force with which they'd been uttered, rocked her.

They stood there looking at each other as the waiting room clock ticked behind them. And then took a steadying breath. Cleared her throat. Got ready to say something that might dispel the energy between them.

But before she could open her mouth, she heard footsteps behind her.

"Ms. Casteele?"

Savannah turned to see a nurse standing there in purple scrubs. "He's all done," she said, smiling. "He's resting now. He did great."

Every nerve ending in Savannah's body heaved a deep sigh. *Thank God...*

"Thank you," she breathed. "Thank you so much."

"Doctor Lieu will be right in, okay?"

She nodded, hearing Judd come up behind her. She probably looked wobbly on her feet. She *felt* wobbly on her feet.

She watched the nurse disappear down the hall. It was over. It was finally over...

Judd touched her elbow and she turned, wanting more than anything to be held while the relief settled in her bones. But wanting him right then felt too risky. If she couldn't do this on her own, where would it stop? When would want turn to need?

Proving something to herself, as much as to him, she stood her ground and simply smiled up at him. How long would it take until his interest in her waned and the reality set in that he was messing with a single mother? Probably not long. Another good reason why she kept her feet planted firmly in place. She *had* to protect herself. As much as she couldn't seem to help flirting with him. And kissing him.

His features, which all too often seemed hard, had softened. He looked genuinely relieved. Happy. And the effect made him more handsome than ever, twisting her heart into a ball of lust, desire, and pain at the thought of *not* going to him. But it was smart, right? That was the smart thing to do.

"I'm gonna go now," he said. "You're going to need this time alone with him. I'm really glad he did so well."

The backs of her eyes stung. But she plowed through. "I bet you'll be one of the first people he'll ask about. You and Maddie."

"She's been texting nonstop. Let him know she's thinking about him, if all the hearts and smiley faces and shit are any indication."

Savannah laughed. "I'll tell him."

"I'll be back in a few days, okay?"

She nodded, not trusting herself to speak. Damn this goodbye. And damn her heart for wrenching like it was.

He reached up and traced her jaw with the tips of his fingers and she almost did crumple then. On the spot.

Swallowing visibly, he stepped around her. And was gone.

Chapter Eleven

SAVANNAH SAT AT the edge of Wyatt's bed, watching him sleep. He was starting to stir, his eyelids fluttering every now and then.

She held his hand, her gaze shifting to the machines which monitored his heartbeat. He looked tiny in the big, white bed, where tubes and wires snaked back and forth. The lower half of his face was slightly swollen, and his lip was covered with a small dressing.

She rubbed her thumb over his knuckles as he tried to open his eyes.

Leaning close, she smoothed his hair with her other hand. "Hey, buddy."

His lids were heavy, but he was determined. He opened them further, his blue eyes unfocussed. But he squeezed her hand with surprising strength, and she smiled.

"It'll take a few minutes to wake up, honey," she said. "Just take your time, okay? I'm not going anywhere."

He blinked at her.

"Maddie says to give you the biggest hug ever," she continued, trying to keep her voice steady. Her poor baby. Her poor, sweet baby. But at the same time, she was so incredibly happy. And grateful this moment was finally here.

At the mention of Maddie, he tried to smile but winced at the effort.

"Aww. I'm very proud of you. You know that?"

He blinked again, his tongue moving over his bottom lip. "I lub you Mamba."

"I love you too, honey. All the ice cream you want, remember?"

"And we can go see da goats? Maddie said maybe we can hab a sleepover soon."

The hopefulness in his voice was killing her. He was already getting attached, and she didn't know what to do about that. Just like she didn't know what to do about the swelling of her heart at the thought of seeing the goats again, of being on the farm again. Of watching Maddie and Wyatt play. Of being in Judd's arms again. It was silly to want those things. They weren't hers. They weren't even guaranteed temporarily. Judd would be going back to work soon, and then everything would change. The farm, the dynamic, the delicate balance they'd come to know over these past few weeks.

"Absolutely," she said, hoping he wouldn't remember this conversation. Because she wasn't in the habit of promising him things she couldn't deliver.

JUDD SAT WITH Maddie on the porch steps, the breeze moving Savannah's spinner around and around. There was a storm moving in. Dark clouds hovered in the distance, promising rain or maybe even hail. The air was heavy and muggy, and smelled sweet, like spring itself.

He looked up at the decorative glass that she'd molded with her own hands, and thought of the way she'd tasted yesterday. How her body had relaxed into his, even though he'd known she hadn't meant to give in so easily. He felt a little guilty about that. He knew she was attracted to him. And he'd normally use that to his advantage. But Savannah was different, and that's where the guilt came in.

"I think you need ducks," Maddie said. She was sipping her lemonade out of a straw, and peering studiously over her glasses to the goats in the pasture. They were eating. Again.

He watched her, trying not to laugh. He thought she was smart and funny and over-the-fucking-moon adorable. But she was also newly sensitive, and whenever he laughed, she thought he was laughing *at* her. And he'd spent more than a few hours trying to get her to come out of the bathroom after saying something that had hurt her feelings, but he could never figure out what the hell it had been.

She was almost thirteen. He and his brothers were broaching new territory, here. Teenage girl territory. Which scared the living shit out of him.

He followed her gaze, where Darryl and Darryl were stuffing their faces to oblivion. "Oh, yeah," he said. "And why's that?"

"I've been reading up on them. They make good pets. They're sweet."

He nodded. He'd never considered a duck's temperament before.

"Did you watch that Dodo video I sent you of that little boy and his duck?" she asked, grinning. Her teeth stuck out a little. She'd need braces soon. "He reminded me of Wyatt."

"I did. Wasn't that a one-legged duck or something?"

"Yeah. He got it caught in a wire when he was a baby."

"Ahh."

"They're so cute. I think you need some. And they could have little ducklings and they could imprint on us and follow us around."

"Uh, no. I'm drawing the line at being a duckling dad."

"Why not? You're a goat dad."

"I'm a goat stepdad. I don't own this place, remember? They're gonna have to go back eventually."

At that, her smile faded and she took another sip of lemonade before chewing on the straw. "Not if you end up buying it."

He watched her, but she didn't look over. He could tell she was on the brink of one of her famous negotiating sessions. She'd convinced Luke to get a dog last winter, and now his ex-army, badass cop brother bought miniature sweaters and went to the doggie park twice a week.

"I'm probably not going to do that, Mads."

"But you could. If you wanted to. Technically."

"Technically I could do a lot of things."

She sighed, breaking his heart with all her awkward angst. She loved this place. He'd wanted that for her. He loved it, too, but owning a farm took a lot of work. More work than one guy who flew all the time could comfortably handle.

"Give me one good reason," she said.

Now they were moving into the nitty-gritty. She was te-nacious as a damn mule. She got that from their mother, who hadn't known when to let go, either. Sometimes it was an endearing trait. Sometimes not.

"Well, for one, I work."

"Lots of people who have farms work."

"Uh-huh. And for another, I'm not a farmer."

"I think you're a great farmer," she said. "You fixed that fence the other day. *And* you gave Darryl his wormer."

It was true. He'd wormed a goat. He'd had to call Lou for directions, then researched it on YouTube just to be safe. And now there seemed to be a bond between man and goat that he didn't really understand, and didn't want to.

"Worming a goat and keeping a farm afloat are two dif-ferent things."

Her lips tilted. "You're a poet and didn't know it."

"Ha. Ha."

"What if you were to…oh, I don't know. Get married, or something. That way there'd be two of you. And come on, Judd. It's not like you have crops to cut down and stuff. Or cows to milk. You make it sound like *Little House on the Prairie* or something."

"Whoa, whoa, whoa." He shifted, dwarfing her in his shadow. "Get *married*?"

She shrugged her thin shoulders.

"Where'd that come from?"

"I have two eyeballs," she said, pushing up her glasses.

"And even though you're my brother, I know you're super cute. And Savannah is super cute, too. And super nice, and she likes it here, and so does Wyatt."

He stared at her. "What?"

"Yeah, okay," she went on in her Dr. Phil tone. "You've always said you're not the *marrying* kind. And I know Mom did a number on you. But you shouldn't let that affect the rest of your life. You really shouldn't."

He didn't know whether to laugh or cry. *What the fuck?* "I…"

"I could be jaded, too," she said. "Like, I like Colton a lot, but I don't know if he likes me back because I'm too skinny—"

"What? You're not too skinny, Mads. You're perfect."

She held up a hand. "I'm too skinny. I know this about myself. And you're my big brother, so you have to say I'm not skinny."

"That's absolutely *not*—"

"Anyhoo, I like him and I don't know if he likes me back. Maybe he doesn't. Or maybe he'll end up being, like, superficial and junk. But I'm not gonna glom onto all Mom's cruddy relationships and project them onto him, because I'm going to give him a chance first."

His mouth hung open.

"We learned about all this stuff in health class," she continued. "Plus, I've been watching *Grey's Anatomy*, so I know about relationships now."

"Since when do you watch *Grey's Anatomy*?"

"Since it's on Netflix, and since Tanner says I can watch

it if I get all my homework done first."

He felt like he needed to talk to Tanner about what was appropriate viewing for a twelve-year-old. Shouldn't she still be watching cartoons or something? He shoved a hand through his hair, suddenly feeling ninety.

"Maddie…"

She patted his knee in a motherly way. "It's okay. You don't have to say anything. Just absorb. Just absorb."

This time he couldn't help it. He laughed.

And she laughed with him.

Chapter Twelve

SAVANNAH PULLED THE fuzzy throw blanket all the way up to Wyatt's chin. Then she fluffed his pillow and coughed again, careful to cover her mouth first.

"Comfy, bud?"

He nodded happily. They'd stayed in front of the pain with his medication, so he didn't seem too uncomfortable, thank goodness. He'd been snuggled in most of the morning, watching *Sponge Bob Square Pants* and sipping strawberry milk.

His lip looked better today. Some of the swelling had gone down, but the itching from the stitches had kicked in, so she'd had to put the fear of Jesus into him not to scratch. They were only four days out from the surgery, and so far recovery had gone without a hitch. Except, of course, for the nasty cold she'd managed to come down with.

She swallowed, wincing at the stab in her tonsils. "Do you need anything else? I might go lie down for a while, okay?"

He reached for her hand and squeezed it. "Okay, Mama."

She leaned down to kiss him, caught herself, and gave

him a hug instead. "I'll be right in the other room, so just holler if you need me."

"I will."

Taking one more look at him, she smiled. But it wasn't without effort. Her head throbbed and her chest burned. *God.* She really couldn't ever remember feeling so awful, and that was factoring in a case of the mumps in the tenth grade. Even the plane ride home with Judd had been overshadowed by feeling crumby. And she hadn't thought anything could overshadow Judd.

She headed down the hallway, mildly tempted to go fold the laundry which had been piling up, or wash the dishes from breakfast, but she was just too exhausted. Every muscle in her body ached, and all she wanted was to crawl in bed for a while. She hadn't really slept since the surgery.

"Mama!"

She froze midstep. Then walked back to the living room and stuck her head in. "Yeah, baby?"

"I spilled my milk. Sorry."

"Oh…" Her feverish gaze settled on the puddle of pink milk that was soaking slowly into the carpet. Her landlord's carpet. She'd have to use some of the money she'd been trying to squirrel away for new brakes to get it cleaned. She felt like crying. "It's okay, honey. I'll get it."

She headed toward the kitchen for some paper towels, feeling dizzy. Putting a hand on the counter to steady herself, she felt her forehead, then her cheeks. She was burning up.

"Mama!" Wyatt called. "Can I have more milk, please?"

Savannah took a shaky breath. "Of course. Just a minute."

Chills sprouted on her arms, then marched their way up her neck and onto her scalp. She was so tired...*so* tired. If she could just get Wyatt settled, maybe he'd nap some. And then she could nap, too.

She tore a wad of paper towels from the holder and wet them down, blinking at the dishes in the sink. She was standing right here and the milk was probably soaked in by now anyway. Might as well get them washed and put away. Then she could clean up the carpet. Then she could lie down. Hopefully.

"Mama?"

She swallowed a whimper before it could escape. "Yeah?"

"My tummy hurts."

Probably from the pain meds, poor kid. They were both a hot mess.

"Okay, honey," she called back. "Maybe milk isn't such a good idea. I'll fix you some ice water, okay?"

"Okay."

Her phone buzzed from the windowsill and she craned her neck to see who it was. *Steven.* He'd had a Facetime call with Wyatt last night. She had to admit, he was making a genuine effort, which was more than he'd made in a long time. But he'd mentioned wanting to visit, and she hadn't been able to reconcile herself to that yet. Facetime was one thing. Having him in their house was something else.

She just didn't have the energy to think about it right now. Her heart was still in a tangle over Judd's last kiss. Her head was foggy from the fever. And her body was dead on its feet. She only had a few more days off, and then she'd have to go back to work, sick or well, tired or rested. Ready or not.

"Mommy?"

She closed her eyes and fought the sensation of falling, falling. *So tired...* "Yes?"

"I love you."

Feeling the sting of tears, she opened them again. Slowly, she lifted her heavy arms and knotted her hair in a messy bun. "I love you too, sweetheart."

Then she stared down at the dishes in the sink. They lay there like skeletons on a battlefield. It seemed like no matter how hard she tried to keep up, she was always losing the war.

The doorbell rang and she jumped. She parted the white, eyelet curtains above the sink and looked out the window. Nothing but the trees blowing in the yard, and a sky full of dark clouds making their way over Copper Mountain in the distance. She couldn't see a car at the curb, so maybe it was a neighbor. Or Mary. She'd said she was dropping by with some soup later, so maybe she'd parked on the other side of the house.

Savannah ran her damp hands down her jeans and made her way toward the front door. Thank God for Mary. The thought of dinner for Wyatt hadn't even made its way past her frontal lobe.

She opened the door, mildly aware that her ears were starting to ache now, too. *Good Lord.* What next?

Looking up, her heart faltered in her chest. Standing there on the porch was Judd.

He watched her through the screen door, his eyes narrowing a little.

Savannah thought she'd normally blush underneath that look, but she was already too warm to feel anything. She put a hand to her hair, self-conscious of how she must look. Like she hadn't showered in two days. Which, well...she hadn't.

"I called a couple of times and you didn't answer," he said. "I was in town and thought I'd come by to check on you two. See how Wyatt's doing."

"That's so sweet." She smiled, her lips dry. "He's doing great. Tired, but great."

"Don't take this the wrong way...but you look pretty tired, too."

That was the understatement of the century.

He stood there, blocking the late afternoon sun poking through the clouds. She tried to focus on his face, but the shards of light surrounding him shot painfully into her eyes. Squinting, she looked away.

"Savannah?"

"I'm okay. I'm—" She swayed, and put a hand against the doorjamb.

Judd jerked the door open and was inside before she knew it. He held her steady with one hand and felt her face with the other. "Jesus," he breathed. "You're on fire. How long have you been like this?"

"It's just a cold," she said. "Er...maybe the flu, I guess. But I'll be okay. I just need to sleep."

"And when were you planning on doing that?"

"I was going to nap when he naps."

Judd looked past her to Wyatt in the living room. "Hey, buddy. How's it going?"

"Good! Mama's gonna clean up my milk. I spilled it."

"Shoot," Savannah muttered. She'd forgotten all about the milk. "It's going to be hard to get that out now. I left it too long."

Judd's gaze settled on her again, and she leaned a little.

"Whoa." He grabbed her hand. "You okay?"

"Kind of dizzy. Just need to rest."

"Mama!" Wyatt called. "Can you come sit with me?"

Savannah's bottom lip trembled before she could help it.

"That's it," Judd said, his voice a low growl. "Come on."

Before she could register, he'd picked her up like a sack of potatoes. Too tired to fight, she let her head flop against his chest. His shirt smelled like fabric softener and aftershave. He was solid and warm, and felt so comforting that she wanted to sob. She didn't know what he was planning on doing with her, but there was a blissful moment of giving herself up to whatever he had in mind.

And then she remembered her son on the couch.

She lifted her head and tried to look over Judd's shoulder. "But Wyatt…"

"It's okay," he said evenly. "I'll watch him while you sleep."

"I can't let you do that."

"So you can prove something? To who? The only thing you're going to accomplish is running yourself into the ground."

He carried her down the hallway, her legs flopping

against his thighs like noodles. They hurt. Her arms hurt. Her head hurt. And now her heart hurt, too.

"Judd, really," she croaked out. "I'm okay. You don't have to do this. You're busy…"

"I'm not too busy to let you collapse from the flu. Nobody expects you to be Superwoman, Savannah. Shut up and let somebody take care of you for once, alright?" The words would've been harsh, except for the tenderness he injected toward the end. So tender that her eyes filled with hot tears. She felt them seep out the corners of her eyes, and make their way down her burning cheeks.

He must've sensed it, because he leaned down and put his lips to her temple. "Shhh, it's okay now," he said. "It's okay."

He made his way into her bedroom and she wasn't too far gone to take a quick inventory of it. Her bed was made, thank God. There were no clothes on the floor, except for a lacy pink bra tossed on the chair by the window. Overall, pretty tidy. For an unexpected visit by a Greek god who was *carrying* her into it. And she couldn't even properly enjoy it because she felt like she'd been run over by a garbage truck.

Balancing her with one arm, he pulled the duvet back, and lay her gently down.

She sighed, her eyelids heavy as books. She looked up at him, not surprised at the reaction her body was having to the bed. As if it had been waiting for this spot, for sleep, for months.

"I—"

Before she could say anything else, he cut her off. "Just a

second, okay?"

She nodded while he pulled the duvet over her. She'd broken out in goose bumps, and the weight, the softness of it felt wonderful against her painful skin.

He walked out of the room, and back down the hallway. She heard him telling Wyatt he'd be staying over a while, and they'd hang out together. Then his heavy footsteps grew fainter as he walked into the kitchen and began opening the cabinets.

After a minute, he came back down the hall and appeared over her bed again, a hunky angel in plaid.

"Here," he said, putting a hand behind her head to lift it up. "Take these."

She plucked the little orange ibuprofens from his palm and tossed them back on her tongue.

"And swallow," he said, holding a glass of water to her lips.

She did as she was told, letting herself lean into his simple directions, his kindness, like she was floating on a river. Down, down she went, letting her arms and legs go limp in warm, serene waters. Letting the heaviness in her eyes win its hard-fought battle, and feeling her lids close like shades against the moonlight.

"Thank…" she heard herself mumble, but couldn't seem to finish.

"Sleep, baby," he said.

And his voice, those words, ushered her into delicious darkness.

Chapter Thirteen

SAVANNAH TURNED HER face into the pillow and breathed deeply, the dream still thick behind her eyes. She'd been walking through an old barn, golden sunlight filtering in through the patched roof. She could smell the hay, see the dust rise in puffs from her boots. And she was looking for someone. Searching, searching, her heart stretched taught with the effort…

And then her reluctant lids fluttered open, and she swallowed, her tonsils telling her to stick it.

Wincing, she scooted up to a sitting position and looked at the clock. She was confused for a few seconds, still groggy with sleep. And then the memory of Judd carrying her down the hall came back with a nudge. He'd given her ibuprofen…he'd stayed with Wyatt so she could sleep.

Almost six hours… That's how long she'd been dead to the world. She heard a muted conversation coming from the living room. One voice deep, and the other light and soft. There was some laughter, then it was quiet again.

Head throbbing, she swung her legs over the side of the bed and sat there for a minute, getting her bearings. Even though she still felt like death warmed over, she felt a little better than she had. But she also felt guilty. Like she'd put Judd out. Like she'd let Wyatt down, which was ridiculous, but she couldn't help it.

She scooted off the bed and stood, running her hands through her hair. She'd just thank Judd profusely. And then she'd call the doctor and hope she could be seen sooner rather than later. She didn't want to miss any more work than she already had. Her bosses were great, but she could be gone only so long without them getting antsy.

She grabbed a sweater from the back of the door, and slipped it on as she made her way down the hall.

Slowing, she smiled as she heard Wyatt giggle again. It sounded like they were playing a game of some sort. Cards, maybe? He loved cards.

She pulled the sweater tight as a fresh crop of chills popped up along her arms.

"Mama!"

Wyatt looked up from the couch. She'd been right—they were playing cards. There was a glass of juice and a half-eaten bowl of soup on the end table. There were also two healthy spots of color on his cheeks and a definitive sparkle in his eyes. He'd needed this.

"Hey, sweetie."

Sitting with his long legs stretched in front of him, was Judd. He looked up too, but his expression was much more guarded. He probably thought she had some kind of contagious jungle virus. He'd actually had to *carry* her to bed, so she didn't end up falling flat on her face.

"Hey, you," he said.

Had he called her baby before? Her belly clenched. Or had that been a fever-induced dream? If so, she'd have to get sick more often.

"Feeling better?" he asked.

She nodded, preparing her tonsils for another assault, then swallowed carefully.

"I am," she said, her voice hoarse. "The sleep was amazing."

"You needed it."

"Are you feeling poorly, Mama?" This from Wyatt who was repeating his favorite Gran-ism.

"A little, honey. But I'll go to the doctor, and then I'll feel better."

Judd watched her. She could see how long his eyelashes were from where she stood. It was ridiculous.

"Mary came by," he said. "She brought the soup and wanted to see how you were."

Savannah chewed on her lower lip for a second. It was dry and chapped. Sore where her teeth grazed it. "Aww, okay. I'll call her later."

Judd leaned forward and put his elbows on his knees. He looked so good, all she could do was stare for a second. His shirt collar gaped open at the throat, and his worn jeans hugged his thighs in a way that made her picture what was underneath. As usual, his sleeves were rolled up to his forearms, where ropy muscle slid under bronzed skin.

Blinking, she looked toward the kitchen, noticing with a squeeze that it was clean, the dishes washed and put away.

"I want you and Wyatt to come stay with me for a few

days," he said. His voice was low and even. Completely matter-of-fact.

She gaped at him.

"I've got plenty of room," he continued, "and Maddie could help with Wyatt, which she'd love."

"I…" Her voice didn't want to cooperate. Or maybe she just didn't want to say no right away.

"You what?"

She cleared her throat, ignoring the ice picks chipping away at her tonsils. "We can't impose on you like that."

"It's not an imposition. I want you there. Maddie wants you there."

"It absolutely *is* an imposition. It's so nice, Judd. But I just can't."

"Give me a reason. Other than it being an imposition, which it's not."

"You've got things to do other than taking care of us."

"Like what? Taking care of Darryl and Darryl?"

"And Frank!" Wyatt interjected.

"Who's Frank?"

Judd remained stony faced. "Maddie's duck. She decided we needed one."

She swallowed back a painful laugh. Maddie had him wrapped around her little finger. "Um…where did you get a duck?"

"Craigslist. His owners had to move into town, and he needed a place to crash."

"So, you're a duck owner."

"A duck foster parent. We're figuring it out as we go.

The point is, I don't start flying again for a few weeks. Which leaves me working on the plane and kicking around an empty farmhouse. Unless Maddie comes over, and then it's just the two of us kicking around an empty farmhouse."

"With two goats and a duck."

"Affirmative."

She smiled at him. She couldn't help being drawn in by this. By all of it. He seemed too good to be true, but *nobody* was perfect. Even Judd Harlow. When was the other shoe going to drop?

Feeling the smile wilt on her lips, she shook her head. "I can't."

He stared up at her. There was a set to his jaw. Like he'd expected an argument, and he wasn't going to have it.

"You're really sick, Savannah," he said, his voice firm. "If you don't want to stay with me, that's okay. I get it. But you should stay with someone. You need help with Wyatt."

He was absolutely right. She had to face the fact that Wyatt needed more than she could provide at the moment. Most basic rule of parenting? You had to be conscious to do it.

"How about Mary?"

"I can't stay with her," she said miserably. "She's too busy with work. I think she's been assigned a story out of state or something, and she's leaving in a few days. She'll be getting ready…I don't want to do that to her."

"Anyone else? Girlfriend? Friend from the office?"

She frowned. There was nobody else. All she did was work and take care of Wyatt. Her social life was nonexistent.

Suddenly, all she could think of was how sad this would make Gran if she knew. She'd be heartbroken. Just like Savannah would be heartbroken to see Wyatt all alone as an adult. Trying but failing to list one damn friend he knew well enough to stay with in a pinch.

The expression on Judd's face softened. "Looks like I'm your best bet, then."

She watched him, her eyes stinging.

"Why don't you go pack some things while Wyatt and I finish up here? Then we'll stop by the urgent care clinic and see if they can get you in. Then we'll head home and bring Mary's soup, and get you better. Okay?"

There were so many things she wanted to say. So many things she wanted to do. Kiss him, for one. Give in to this feeling unfurling inside her, for another. But she stopped herself before she could. Before she could feel any more of the layers around her heart being peeled away. Because she actually needed those.

So she nodded instead. "Okay."

JUDD LIFTED THE lid from the pan. Steam hit him directly in the face, along with the mouthwatering smell of sizzling beef.

He'd never made calzone before, but it had been one of his favorite comfort foods as a kid. His mom hadn't been present much during his childhood, emotionally or otherwise, but one of her biggest strengths had been her cooking. Jesus, she'd been an amazing cook. Able to pull something together when their cupboards had been almost bare. She'd excelled at that.

It was a talent Judd had come to realize some people had, or they didn't. Jennifer Harlow hadn't had a mother to teach her. She'd learned on her own, which made it even more impressive. He got that now, where as a teenager his anger for her had been so blinding, he hadn't been able to stand back and see her for who she really was—flawed and complicated. It had helped humanize her, letting him come to a place of slow forgiveness.

In fact, it was her cookbook he was working out of now. Her notes in the margins, her dog-eared pages, her highlighted sections. It was the one thing he'd wanted of hers when she'd died. That, and her wedding ring. He hadn't understood why it had been important to him at the time, since her first marriage had been a bitter mess, but he'd wanted it just the same. Maybe because the single diamond had looked so hopeful sparkling from her jewelry box. Like it never really had a chance, but didn't know how to give up.

Maddie sat on the barstool at the island, her worn sneakers squeaking on the footrest.

"Can I taste the sauce?" she asked. "I'm *starving.*"

He dipped a spoon into the bubbling pan and put it up to her mouth, one hand ready to catch any drips. "Blow on it. It's hot."

She took a careful taste, and his chest tightened. She looked more like Tanner than anyone in the family, but every now and then she reminded him of their mom. She had her eyes. The same sharp wit.

"It's yummy," she said.

"Righteous."

She wrinkled her nose at his attempt at teenager. He'd missed the mark by about twenty years, but whatever.

"You look funny in that apron," she said.

He looked down. "This? I think it makes me look like I know what I'm doing."

"It makes you look like a grandma. Who needs a shave."

"Ouch?"

Smiling, she spun the stool completely around before planting her hands on the counter to stop it. "Okay. I'm gonna sit with Wyatt for a while before dinner. I promised him we'd play Go Fish."

"Good girl."

"And Savannah's still sleeping. Should we wake her?"

"Nah. Let her sleep. She needs it."

"Judd?"

Her gaze settled on him meaningfully. He stopped stirring the sauce and looked at her. "Yeah?"

"I think it's really cool that you asked them to stay here."

He smiled, noticing again how much she was growing up. Her hair was longer than it'd been last summer. And she'd gained a little weight. Not much, but a little. She was changing some every day, and it did something to him. In his heart she'd probably always be a toddler with skinned knees and a lisp, but he also knew he'd have to eventually accept the young woman, too. Someone with her own ideas and feelings about things.

"I'm glad you think so, Mads," he said, stirring the sauce

again. "But it's easy to invite Savannah and Wyatt here because they're so great. It's harder to remember to be kind when people aren't so great. I want you to always be kind, no matter what. No matter the circumstances, okay?"

She nodded, serious. She'd always been a good listener. Like a little sponge, soaking it all in.

"What does philanderer mean?"

Judd froze. "What?"

"Philanderer."

"Where'd you hear that?"

"One of the girls in my prealgebra class said it. When I told her I was babysitting for Wyatt. She said his dad left because he's a philanderer."

"Ahh." Judd felt the muscles in his shoulders tense. "First of all, don't listen to that kind of talk, Maddie. I'm guessing most people who would say something like that don't know the whole story. At least not from Savannah herself. Secondly, don't ever join in. Wyatt's too young to know what people are saying now, but someday he will. It's never any fun to have your family's business dragged through the mud." He said this last part while watching her intently. Because if there was one thing the Harlow kids understood, it was this.

"I won't," she said, her voice soft.

He nodded.

"But what does it mean?"

Judd frowned. Then took a deep breath. "It means a man who sleeps with a lot of women."

"Oh."

He could see the wheels turning behind the reflection of her glasses, and braced himself for the next question.

"Judd?"

"Yeah."

"Was my dad a philanderer?"

Judd put the spoon on the counter and turned down the heat under the skillet. Then walked around to where Maddie sat on the stool and pulled her close. She immediately lay her head against his chest, something she'd done since babyhood.

"Your dad could never commit to Mom, Maddie. Just like my dad couldn't commit to her. I guess you could say both our dads were philanderers."

She sniffed. He wondered if she was crying. Hoped she wasn't, but her shoulders were shaking a little. Damn that bastard to hell. Judd had long since accepted not having a father of his own. But Maddie had always missed hers, had never given up hope that he'd come back for her.

"I remember them fighting about a lady named Betsy," Maddie said. "Before Daddy moved out. It was a bad one. He threw the TV and broke it."

Judd and Luke had moved out by then, but he remembered Betsy and her trail of scorched earth well enough. Tanner and Maddie had lived through that one in Technicolor. So many fights, so many affairs, so many broken moments in their family.

"Yeah," he said against her hair. "He used to throw a lot of things, didn't he?"

Maddie nodded.

After a minute, he took her by the shoulders and pulled her away enough to look at her. There were streaks of tears down her cheeks, but her expression was sadly resigned. And that crushed something inside of him.

"Your dad didn't deserve you, Maddie," he said. "And as screwed up as Mom was sometimes, he didn't deserve her, either. It's important you understand, now that you're a little older."

She nodded again.

"He kept messing up and she kept taking him back," he continued. "She never should've done that because it fucked up your childhood. And Tanner's. Shit…sorry for swearing."

She smiled. "It's okay."

"But he treated her badly, and I don't want you growing up thinking that's what a woman deserves. You deserve to be treated with love and respect, and if a boy doesn't give you that, you tell him to take a hike, got it? A long walk off a short pier. Period."

She looked up at him, her nose running. She dabbed it with the back of her hand. "I get it. But Mom said she loved him."

Judd remembered that, too. And how the second chances had turned into thirds. And the thirds, fourths. And on and on and on.

"I know she loved him," he said. "But sometimes love isn't enough. Sometimes you can't love a person enough for the both of you. Good, healthy relationships don't work that way. It's a two-way street. And Mom wanted to be with someone so bad, that she almost always loved too much, and got loved too little in return. Your dad, my dad, all her boyfriends over the years, they never loved her like she should've been loved. And instead of finding that love and acceptance in you, and in Tanner and Luke and me, she couldn't stop looking for it in guys she barely knew."

Maddie's face crumpled then, and she let out a choking sob. "I hated that about her."

Judd pulled her back against his chest, each sob like a knife to his gut. "I know, Mads. Me too. But she couldn't help it. And I think when someone dies, when they go to heaven, everything is like it should be again. Everything they struggled with goes away. And there's just…peace."

Maddie took in a shaky breath, and let it out slowly. After a minute, she'd grown still again and pulled away to wipe her face. "I like that," she said. "I like thinking Mama's at peace."

He hadn't heard her say Mama in a long time. It was a small, tender spot that had been exposed. He wished he could shield her from everything that could hurt her, push away every person who might try and find that tender spot and use it against her. But he'd never be able to protect her from it all. The best thing he could do as her big brother, that Tanner and Luke could do too, was teach her. And raise her to be a strong woman who valued herself enough to demand to be treated with respect. And love.

"You know what else I think?" Judd asked, pushing her hair away from her face.

"What?"

"I think Mom watches over you every day, Mads. And I

think she's so proud of you."

There was a spark behind her eyes. The lighting of something special. He'd seen it before. It was his job to keep blowing gently, gently, until it caught fire.

"You do?" she said.

"I really do."

Chapter Fourteen

SAVANNAH COULDN'T REMEMBER the last time she'd gotten to sit on the couch and watch an entire movie. At least not a movie that wasn't for the under-five crowd.

She burrowed deeper into the Sherpa blanket that Judd had covered her with a few minutes ago and set the remote on the end table beside her hot tea and cough drops. He'd told her to pick a movie and he'd watch it with her. So naturally she'd gone straight for *Sleepless in Seattle*, which she'd paused during the opening credits so he wouldn't miss anything.

Smiling, she listened to Judd and Wyatt in the bathroom. It was teeth brushing time, which as a mom, she'd always found daunting. Somehow it took close to twenty minutes every night. It was like stepping inside some kind of wormhole.

But Judd seemed to be handling it like a pro. She could hear him explaining the difference between flying jets, and flying prop planes. This, in between telling Wyatt to open wider, and rinse.

"Okay, wipe your mouth buddy," he said.

"I want to ride bucking horses. But maybe I could fly

planes, too."

"I think you can do anything you want."

"Anything?"

"Anything," Judd said. "You be good to your mama, and study hard in school, and the sky's the limit."

"Would you teach me to fly a plane, Judd? When I get to be growed up?"

Someone turned off the faucet and it was quiet for a minute. Savannah waited, her chest tight. She swallowed, but barely registered the pain in her tonsils. It was her heart that seemed to be the most tender part of her right now.

"When you get to be grown up, I'll teach you to fly, kiddo," Judd said. "If you still want to fly, I'll teach you."

Savannah let out a breath she hadn't realized she'd been holding. She didn't know what she'd expected him to say. That he might not be around when Wyatt was grown up? That he might just be a distant memory? Of course not. But the sweet way he answered touched her just the same.

After a few seconds, Judd appeared with Wyatt on his shoulders. He walked over and leaned down so Wyatt could wrap his little arms around her neck.

"Night, Mama. Judd doctored my lip."

"Oh, good. Did it hurt?"

"Nope!"

As Judd straightened again, she caught his gaze. And there was something unspoken between them. Something she didn't know if she could verbalize if she'd tried. Her heart swelled, even as she willed it not to. She saw visions of a family, a whole family, and she pushed them away again before they could take root.

"I'm gonna tuck this slugger in and I'll be right back." He turned to the TV and his lips tilted. "I see it's going to be death by chick flick."

She laughed, trying not to let it turn into a coughing fit. "You said any movie."

"Damn. I did say that."

He winked at her and walked out of the room leaving her ovaries aching along with every muscle in her body.

When he came back, she was stretched out, but pulled her feet up to make room.

He sat and put his hand on her knee. "You good? Want more tea?"

"No, I'm great. Thank you. You're the best nurse, Judd. And the best teeth brusher, apparently."

"What can I say? Get the kid talking about planes..."

"Right?"

His gaze settled on her, taking her in. And her cheeks warmed under it.

"You sure you're doing okay?" he asked. "How are you feeling?"

"Better, I think." She smoothed the blanket over her lap like it was some kind of cocktail dress. "I've never had anyone take care of me like this. Never. In my whole life."

He frowned. "Come on. Your mom must've."

"She got by with the basics. But when it came to comfort, my dad always filled that space."

"Well, that's something at least."

"It was. I loved him a lot. When he was home."

"What about your husband?" His voice was low. Guttural. He reached out and smoothed the hair away from her face.

"Oh. Well…nursing wasn't exactly his specialty."

He watched her.

"He went out with his buddies the night we brought Wyatt home from the hospital," she continued. "Didn't come back until dawn. I just remember being so exhausted because Wyatt had trouble latching on, of course. He cried and cried. And then I started crying, too. And we spent the whole night like that. Walking the floor and crying."

"Jesus."

She shrugged. Like it was nothing, like it didn't mean as much as it did. Another defense mechanism. But that was crap, because it did mean something. That night four years ago was the first moment she realized the life she'd wanted for her son probably wasn't going to become a reality.

"It is what it is," she said. "That which does not kill us makes us stronger, right?"

"Something like that."

"It has made me stronger. Doesn't mean I don't wish things were different sometimes, but Wyatt's loved, and he knows that."

Judd was quiet for a minute, running his hand over her legs.

"I remember Maddie being sick one time when she was a toddler," he said. The room was so hushed, she could hear Wyatt's soft snores from the bedroom. "My mom was on a bender, and my stepdad wasn't around. I've never seen a kid so sick in my life. She couldn't stop throwing up. I had to call a cab to take us to the ER." He looked over and smiled. "That was a low point. Nobody should ever feel abandoned like that. Ever. But I agree with you. It made me stronger, too."

She reached for his hand and he took it. They sat there on the couch, the movie on pause across the living room. The house seemed to be breathing softly, too, right along with Wyatt. Along with Savannah, who felt like she was waiting for something, but didn't know what.

A feeling of complete and utter warmth settled over her then. A feeling of protection, of sweet repose. She squeezed his hand, wanting to remember this moment. Because no matter what happened in the days and weeks to come, she knew she'd always compare other people in her life to this man, and how he was making her feel right then.

Judd stretched his long legs out in front of him and sighed. "I have to be honest here. This is the part where I'd say screw the movie, and kiss the girl instead."

She smiled slowly.

"But since you're still kind of puny, I'm gonna resist and go make some popcorn. Sound good?"

She laughed. Then coughed. "Sounds good. And Judd?"

"Yeah."

"Thank you."

SAVANNAH PUT HER hands deep in the pockets of her

sweater, and walked down the hallway, her bare feet padding on the hardwood floor. Shafts of early morning sunlight shown in through the single-pane windows of the farmhouse, adding to its cozy feel. She could smell a fire burning in the fireplace, bacon sizzling from the stove—something to take the edge off the chilly spring morning.

It was Saturday, marking a full week since she and Wyatt had come to stay with Judd, and her stomach tightened at the realization. They'd stayed too long. She'd started getting better days ago, and now sleeping over felt less like a kindness bestowed, and more like something else completely. And the problem was, she was beginning to fall in love with that something else completely. The house, the gangly tween who thought of herself as Wyatt's teacher and playmate. And the man who had taken her little family in.

She slowed as she looked up at the pictures lining the hallway. Judd and his brothers as little boys. His mother as a young woman. Maddie as a toddler, tiny for her age, and with the biggest, roundest eyes Savannah thought she'd ever seen.

She touched her throat absentmindedly, as if expecting a lump to form there. Not surprising, since she'd done a lot of crying these last few weeks. Anticipation, stress, anxiety, had all taken their toll.

But here, now, she didn't feel any of those things. What she felt was a deep and profound contentment at being in this house. *Joy* in being welcomed by its family. Love at belonging, for however short the stay might be. And it didn't take a therapist to tell her this was what she'd been longing for her entire damn life.

Maybe that's why she was feeling for a lump. The ache she knew would eventually take over when she and Wyatt left. And they'd need to leave soon. It wasn't her place to be feeling these things, and it wasn't fair of Judd to be offering them. It wasn't realistic. Families didn't just *happen* like this. They had to be made, built. And it took a lot more time than just one magical week recovering from bronchitis.

"My ears stuck out a little, but I think I grew into them."

She turned to see Judd standing a few feet away, hands in his pockets, a dish towel thrown casually over one shoulder.

Smiling, she crossed her arms over her chest.

"You definitely grew into them. And that serious look of yours." She glanced back at a picture of him around fourteen or so, one lanky arm thrown around Luke. They were standing knee-deep in a snowdrift and Luke was giving the photographer a toothy grin. But not Judd. He looked like he was calculating his taxes in his head.

He laughed. "Yeah, I didn't look very happy, did I?"

"I just think you looked...older than your age."

A darkness passed over his features, but then it vanished. Like he was used to masking pain, or disappointment, or longing. Or all of the above.

"We can thank my dad for that," he said, his voice even. "I was the man of the house by the eighth grade. Didn't leave much time for football and girls."

Savannah watched him, her heart hurting for the boy in the picture. Sad for his lost childhood, and sad for her own. But while Judd hadn't had time to wallow in his father's leaving, she'd never stopped pining away for hers.

"I always wanted a little brother or sister," she said quietly. "You were lucky in that way at least."

After a few long seconds, he nodded. "What happened with your mom? You never mention her."

"That's because we don't really talk. She moved away about five years ago to get remarried, and she doesn't have much interest in Wyatt, so…"

"I'm sorry."

"Don't be. We've got my gran, and she's amazing."

"I'm sure she is."

"I should take you to meet her sometime."

"I'd like that."

She pulled in a slow breath. *What are you even doing, Savannah?* Did she just suggest taking him to meet her grandmother? She was in so deep, she worried she wouldn't be able to climb back out again. And what exactly was that going to mean for her heart in the long run? And for Wyatt's?

"Judd…" she began.

He was standing so close now that she could see the individual points of stubble on his chin. And a tiny scar across his right eyebrow.

"What?"

"I don't know that I'll ever be able to thank you enough for what you did." She waved her hand in a wide arc. "This, this…whole thing. Taking us in, cooking for us, making sure we've been taken care of this week. You couldn't have been nicer if you were our own family."

"I wanted to do it."

She frowned, wanting an explanation, a *real* explanation for the first time since they'd walked in the door.

"But why?" she continued. "We're not family. You barely even know us. Why are you doing this?"

"Because I like you. I like Wyatt. I think you could use a break for once."

"But a break would be bringing us pizza. Or a gift certificate for a massage. Not inviting us to stay with you for an entire week."

He shrugged as if it was nothing.

She felt her expression harden before she could help it. That old pride rising up before she could yank it back down and make it behave. "You don't have to feel sorry for us. We're okay. We're doing okay."

He looked unfazed. "I don't feel sorry for you. And I can tell you're doing okay."

"Then why?"

"Wow. You really need a hard and fast reason, don't you?"

She stared up at him.

"What if I said I wanted to sleep with you?"

"Nice try," she said dryly. "You didn't have to put us up for a week to accomplish that."

He raised his brows.

"I mean, hypothetically."

Judd's gaze fell and took her in. All of her, before her face warmed and she wrapped the cardigan around herself like a shield.

His eyes locked on hers. "You really need a reason other than I'm totally fucking hot for you?"

She nodded, feeling stubborn. Feeling turned on. Feeling, what exactly, she didn't know. Heartsick? Because no matter how hard she tried to see the outcome of this scenario, it always ended badly. She'd been down this road before.

"I admire you," he said evenly.

"You admire me."

"Is that so hard to believe?"

"No…" She worried her lip for a second before letting out a breath. "Maybe?"

"You remind me a lot of *me*, Savannah. How I was as a kid, taking care of my brothers and sister by myself."

"But I'm not a kid."

"No, you're not. But you're pretty young and you're shouldering all of this alone."

"I'm no different than millions of other single parents."

"Jesus. Why are you so hesitant to accept some praise?"

It was true. She was hesitant. "Because you say these things, Judd. You say these things and it makes me want to…"

"Makes you want to what?"

Rip that shirt off. Bite your nipples. Suck on your earlobes…

She ran a frustrated hand through her hair. "You can't say these things, all these nice things, and expect me not to fall for you. You can't make a calzone for me, and tuck me in at night when I have a fever, play card games with my kid, and expect me not to fall in love with you."

Oh, God…Oh, God… The words were out and hanging

between them before she'd realized what she'd done.

Her heart pounded, her ears burned. This was why it'd been stupid to stay this long. *Stupid, stupid, stupid.* It would've made more sense if she *had* ripped off his shirt and bitten his nipples. But she'd gone batshit crazy and used the L-word instead. The *L-word.*

"I…" She didn't even know what to say. Nothing fit. The look on his face was almost worse than what had just come out of her mouth. Like she'd poured ice water over his head.

And then she remembered this was his fault, anyway. If he hadn't been so damn wonderful, none of this would've happened. But he had been wonderful. He'd been kind, and charming, and almost perfect.

She squared her shoulders, which wasn't easy. She wanted to push past him and crawl into a hole.

"You had to have known this was going to happen," she said. "Are you *trying* to make me fall for you?"

And then the thought occurred to her that maybe he *was* trying, but had overshot miserably. Maybe he really was doing this to get her to sleep with him.

"Stop," he said, stepping close. "Just stop. Okay?"

Her gaze dropped to his lips, to the slight cleft in his chin. And she was toast.

He lowered his head, and his beautiful mouth was on hers.

He pushed her up against the wall. She felt the pictures at the back of her head, and was careful not to knock them sideways as she struggled not to come right out of her skin.

His big hands settled on her hips as he urged her mouth open with his tongue. He was warm and wet, salty and sweet, fast and slow all at the same time.

Her heart dropped any pretense of civility, and hammered like a wild thing inside her chest. She could feel the pulse behind her ears, tapping out a hot, primal rhythm. The delicate spot between her legs pulsed, too. Her entire body was electrified by his touch.

She reached up and ran her hands through his hair, feeling the thick, silky tendrils slide between her fingers. He responded by grinding into her, leaving no doubt he wanted more than just a few stolen seconds in the hallway.

He smelled so good and she breathed deep, wanting to saturate her lungs with him. She slid her hands down his neck, across his broad shoulders, down over his arms. She could feel the tendons straining underneath his warm skin, the energy of the bulging muscle over bone.

He was absolutely huge. Just his physical presence should've intimidated her, maybe even scared her. But he had the opposite effect. She felt as safe as she ever had in her life.

God, she craved more of that feeling. More of *him*, period. And the realization was unsettling.

Putting both hands on his chest, she gave a shaky push.

Slowly, reluctantly, he broke the kiss. But it didn't seem without effort. He touched his forehead to hers and made a low, frustrated sound.

"The kids are just outside," she said. It was true, they were. But that wasn't the reason she'd pushed him away. He was making her imagine things she'd convinced herself she didn't need right now—sex, desire, love...

But what if she got them? Just what if? *Judd naked. Judd saying her name in her ear. Judd picking her up and cradling her against him...* It was almost too much to bear. She longed for those things. But she railed against them, too. *She* was in charge of making herself feel safe and loved. She'd spent too long trying to find her strength after Steven had left to lose it now. And it was a bitter pill to swallow knowing deep down she was forcing herself to choose between strength and happiness.

The screen door slammed and little footsteps clomped toward the kitchen. "Just getting some water, Mama!" Wyatt called.

Judd moved away, one hand lingering on her hip for a second, before he took that, too. Her heart ached at the chill it left behind.

As if reading her thoughts, he reached up and smoothed her brow.

"I could give you what you want, Savannah," he said quietly.

She swallowed hard. That was the problem.

She wanted it all.

Chapter Fifteen

J UDD STOOD LOOKING into the old plane's engine with the
duck between his feet. He nudged it with his boot, earning
an indignant quack.

"Beat it, Frank."

Frank waddled over between two hay bales, shook out
his fluffy, white butt, and settled down like he was going to
lay an egg.

Judd stared at him. He was a precocious little thing. He
wasn't scared of anything, and had never met a human he
didn't like. Maddie was getting worried some overzealous
hunter might take a shot at him, so Judd tried to keep him in
the barn while he was working. It was like having a damn
dog with feathers. And an entitlement complex.

"Comfy?"

Frank stared back, his shiny black eyes like two new buttons. Then quacked before tucking his orange bill neatly
underneath his wing.

Judd smiled, turning back to the engine. He was getting
closer and closer to getting the plane in flying shape. Pretty
soon he'd be able to haul it out to the airport with the 340.
He'd been smart over the years with his salary and some

well-timed investments, so the thought that maybe he'd bitten off more than he could chew with two planes hadn't really sunk in until now. But to be fair, he'd been preoccupied lately. Very preoccupied.

Savannah and Wyatt were leaving tomorrow, something that was turning him inside out. It had been only a week, but he'd gotten used to their sweet presence in the house. He found he liked having someone to look over, a little kid to run barefoot down the hallway, a beautiful woman's things strewn out over the bathroom counter.

The entire house smelled like coconut now. And baby shampoo. Their scent, their very *essence* seemed to have permeated the walls. And maybe even Judd's walls too. Because never in his life had he thought about settling down like he was thinking about it now. What it might be like, how it would work... All the intricate details of family life.

But at the end of the day, he had to keep reminding himself why he hadn't gone there before. Because families, the kind with a mom and dad, and well-adjusted kids, fell apart. They always fell apart.

Frowning, Judd wiped his hands on a rag, then tossed it on the plane's wing. Savannah had been absolutely right to call him on his bullshit. He was tempting fate. Tempting her. And tempting himself, too. This wasn't a game. She deserved someone who could give all of himself, and not just the parts he could spare without too much risk.

He looked toward the house as a flock of Canadian geese passed over, honking their right-of-way. She'd taken Wyatt into town to pick up some groceries at Monroe's Market.

She'd said she wanted to make something special for dinner, something to thank Judd for what he'd done. He'd tried to discourage it. She was still recovering and he didn't want her overdoing it. But she'd insisted.

Frank poked his head out from underneath his wing and craned his neck. Then Judd heard it, too. The sound of his truck rumbling up the dirt road.

He stood there waiting, recognizing the quickening of his heartbeat. He wasn't used to this kind of anticipation. These weird nerves. When it came to women, Judd didn't have to work at it. He never had. Even in high school, his size alone had been a blessing in that area, and he'd always just taken girls' interest in him for granted.

But he was learning with Savannah, he couldn't take anything for granted. She wasn't the kind to be easily swayed, he'd seen that the very first day. She smiled easily, but had a pensive soul. She was always thinking, always planning, always worried about the what-ifs. He had a feeling sleeping with him was on some kind of forbidden list she'd made for herself.

Turning back to the Skyhawk, he heard the truck come to a stop outside. After a second, the door slammed and footsteps made their way toward the barn.

He looked over his shoulder to see her walk inside. The late afternoon sun shone behind her, tinging her hair in gold. It was down today, and the color that had been missing from her cheeks last week was back. She looked flushed, pretty. Her green eyes clear and bright.

She smiled, and glanced away. Probably because he was

staring. Like he wanted to rip that sheer white blouse off and watch the buttons go flying. Which, he did. But he didn't necessarily want her knowing that. *Jesus.*

He turned back to the plane out of pure necessity. All of a sudden his jeans felt too tight.

Picking up a wrench, he looked into the plane's dusty engine.

"Where's Wyatt?" he asked.

She came up next to him, her feet rustling over the straw. Frank got up and waddled over, quacking out a welcome.

"Well, hi, there, Frank. Have you been helping?" She bent to pat the duck's little head and straightened again. "Wyatt's in town. I stopped at the studio to pick up a few supplies and ran into Tanner and Maddie outside. They were heading to the park and asked if Wyatt could come. Doctor Lieu said as long as he's up to playing, I should let him. He's healing so fast. He really looks great, doesn't he?"

Judd nodded, not trusting himself to look over again. He liked to think of himself as a decent guy. But he was no saint, either. And they were alone for the first time in a long time. And he could smell her perfume on the thick afternoon air.

"Better than great," he said.

Out of the corner of his eye, he could see her cross her arms over her chest. He imagined her breasts pressed together, a dark, sweet crevice between them.

Leaning over the engine, he looked for any damn thing to distract him. Prayed for *something* to distract him.

"I bought the makings for my gran's eggplant Parmesan,"

she said. "The best in three counties."

"Sounds good. I'm starving."

He could feel the weight of her gaze on his shoulders. Ever since he'd met her he'd wanted her closer, closer. But right now, he only wanted her somewhere else. Away from him. Away from what he might be tempted to do if she stood there much longer. Because where exactly would this go between them? Was he prepared to offer her anything other than sex? Sure, he'd had fleeting thoughts of more. But the reality was a sharp wire tangled around his feet. And if he ever forgot, his childhood was always there to remind him when he was tempted to take a step forward.

He heard her pull in a breath, then let it out slowly. "The light in here is beautiful. So peaceful. It's a perfect place to work."

Frank waddled out the barn door quacking to himself as he went, and left them alone in the suddenly heavy silence.

"Uh-huh."

"How's it going?" she asked after a few seconds. "With the plane?"

"Fine."

Now he was just being a dick. But he honestly couldn't turn to her and pretend to have a light conversation when his chest was this tight.

She rocked forward on her ballet slippers. He only knew they were called ballet slippers because Maddie had roughly ten pair that she left all over the living room floor for him to trip over. Savannah's were electric blue and showed enough of her foot that it made him want to slip them off and rub his thumb over her delicate, white skin.

"Are you mad at me?" she asked.

"What? No. No, I'm not mad."

She was quiet, and he hoped to God she'd just let it go.

"Because you seem like it," she finally said.

He knocked the wrench against the inside of the engine on accident, and the sharp sound made her jump.

"Well, I'm not."

He still didn't look at her. But she remained planted there. Stubborn. Demanding something from him that he should've demanded from himself a long time ago. Accountability.

"Are you upset about what happened earlier?" she asked.

What happened earlier... She was going to have to be more specific. There were about a hundred things wreaking havoc with his brain at the moment, all of them having to do with her. None of them her fault.

"Earlier?"

She rocked forward on those shoes again. A nervous habit. He was making her nervous. Normally that could work to his advantage, but in this case, it made him feel shitty.

"When we...kissed," she said.

"Why would that make me upset?" He did turn to her then, tossing the wrench back in the toolbox. A little too hard. He really was fucking this moment up royally.

She raised her chin. "Because I pushed you away, remember?"

How could he forget?

"I wasn't upset, Savannah."

"I just thought…" Her voice trailed off.

"I wasn't upset," he said again. This time quieter. "Disappointed, maybe. But I'd never be upset with you for not wanting more."

She laughed.

"What?"

"Is that what you think?"

He narrowed his eyes at her. Trying to figure her out. Not knowing if that'd be such a good thing, because she had more than a few layers. What was he planning on doing when he got down to the ones that really made her tick?

"Are you saying you *did* want more?"

"No," she said.

His heart sank in his stupid, cavernous chest. "Gotcha."

"I mean no, that's past tense."

"What's past tense?"

"The word *did*. The right word is *do*."

He watched her steadily. "Savannah…"

"I *do* want you. Now. Currently. Current tense."

Jesus. He never thought correct grammar could get him hard, but he was wrong.

He stood there fighting the urge to go to her. To pick her up, and lay her down in the hay, and move over her like he'd imagined doing about a hundred times so far. He fought it because he knew she was at war with herself. And she was vulnerable. And that dictated he stay absolutely still, despite it being one of the hardest things he'd ever done.

"I sense a but coming," he said.

"I have to consider Wyatt in everything I do, Judd. And

if I sleep with you, I'm going to go ahead and fall all the way. And if I fall all the way, I'm going to have to pick myself off the floor when you tell me you're not ready for anything serious, which I know you're probably not. I mean, we've only known each other a few weeks, for God's sake. But I can't help how I feel…how I'm starting to feel about you."

He nodded. "Okay. I get that. I understand."

Her face crumpled and she stomped her foot. "*See?* That's what I'm talking about. That right there."

"What?"

"Do you ever say the wrong thing? Ever? It'd be so much easier if you were an asshole."

"I am an asshole. Ask my brothers."

"No, they adore you. Everyone adores you. Because you're amazing."

"You have to stop putting me on some kind of unrealistic pedestal. I'm just a guy. And I'm not perfect."

She frowned. "No. I know you're not. But you're perfect to me."

Now, that should've scared the shit out of him. It really should've. But the look on her face was such a mixture of tenderness and embarrassment, that he wanted to pull her close and kiss every single inch of her.

"Savannah, baby," he said, his voice low. "I want you. I'm dying for it. But I'm not going to make the first move here. You're gonna have to do that. Whatever happens, I don't want you to regret it."

She nodded. "So you're giving me complete control."

"Yes."

"I've never had control over anyone before."

"Right now you could tell me to drop to my knees, and I would."

She chewed the inside of her cheek, and he caught a glimpse of her tongue.

"So I have to decide to live with the consequences..."

He didn't want to be a consequence for her. But she was being smart. Smarter than him.

She hooked her thumbs in her jean pockets. "I guess blaming this whole thing on Wyatt isn't fair."

He didn't say anything. He was afraid if he did, he might break the fragile web forming between them. Linking them together in a commonality of fear and desire.

"Most of it does have to do with him," she said. "But a lot has to do with me, too. How I grew up. How Steven left. I can't let that happen again. Because I want a family so bad, it terrifies me."

She smiled, but looked close to tears. "And I know that no woman in her right mind would be saying this to a man she was interested in because it'd make him run in the opposite direction. But if I'm in control, I have to be honest, even if it does make you want to run."

He swallowed with some difficulty. His entire throat was dry now. "I'm not going anywhere."

"Because you want to sleep with me. And I get that, because I want to sleep with you, too. But it's not the same as knowing you're ready to start a relationship with someone."

"I don't think it's fair to assume what I'm ready for and what I'm not. You haven't asked me shit."

She cocked her head, and he knew he was going to have to tread lightly here. Because he didn't want to run, that was true. But she was right—wanting to sleep with someone was entirely different than wanting to settle down.

"Don't worry," she said. "I'm not going to back you into a corner with a question like that."

"Savannah…" He sighed. "I'm trying to figure things out right now. Not just with you, but with me. My life. How I feel about my mom, even though she's gone. About my dad, and how being related to him makes me worry I'll turn out exactly fucking like him."

She frowned, her eyes bright.

He looked down at his boots, composing himself. Because choking up in front of her was *not* how he'd pictured this going.

When the ache had eased from his throat, he looked back up. "Those things you want? The family? The stability? The life? I want those things, too. I always have, even though I haven't admitted it until now. Even to myself. But the point is, you and I…we're not that different."

She took a step toward him. A slow step. What looked like a tentative step. Her expression was raw, probably because it mirrored his own. Was it possible that she'd come into his life to complete it? Judd didn't know if he believed in things like that. He sure as hell hadn't before. But the look on her face, the warmth in her eyes made him question everything he thought he'd understood about himself. She'd turned him upside down.

A few more steps, and she was standing in front of him.

So close that he could smell the lotion on her skin. Her face was scrubbed clean, emphasizing the haphazard freckles scattered across her nose.

She pulled her bottom lip between her teeth like she was trying for the right words. He could empathize. He'd never been a smooth a talker. But he would've given anything right then to say something poetic. Something worthy of how he felt—like he was looking directly into the sun, feeling it on his bare arms after being cooped up after a long, cold winter.

But as luck would have it, he didn't need to say anything at all. Because she reached up and pressed her palms against his chest. Then stood on her tiptoes, and kissed him.

Chapter Sixteen

SAVANNAH'S HEART GALLOPED inside her chest. Her hands were shaking against his pecs. But she was beyond stopping herself now. She didn't want to think anymore, didn't want to weigh the options, or calculate the odds of getting hurt. Or worse, of Wyatt getting hurt. She just wanted to feel good. To feel loved for a few precious minutes.

She wanted to be carried away, and she wanted Judd to be the one carrying her. She hadn't planned on this. In fact, she'd been planning on walking away before anything serious happened between them. Until the second he'd opened up and she'd seen the naked emotion on his face. *Of course* he'd always wanted a family. Why wouldn't he? When his father had abandoned him just like Savannah's had abandoned her? They were both guarded about it, but in a different way. She longed for it more openly, while his longing lay underneath the surface, like small ribbons of gold throughout a rock. Today was the first day she could see the glint of it, the sparkle on an otherwise dark surface. And Lord help her, she felt an undeniable connection that had drawn her in. She felt powerless to it. And she wouldn't have wanted to fight it anyway. At least not today.

He leaned down slowly, so tenderly that it nearly broke her heart, and wrapped one massive arm around her lower back. No matter how many times she kissed Judd, she never tired of the feeling of him grounding her. Like she was a sapling that had been struggling in a storm, and had only now found purchase in the soil.

She slid her hands up his chest, her entire body trembling now. With nerves, because she hadn't done this in a very long time. But also with desire. A distinctive ache that needed soothing. A hunger that needed satiated. All of a sudden she couldn't remember a time when she hadn't wanted Judd.

He pressed his mouth against hers. And then his tongue was tracing the inside of her lips. His arm tightened around her. She could feel his erection against her hip, and she lifted her leg, wrapping it around the back of his knee.

He groaned and went rigid for a second, before pulling away enough to look down at her. His eyes were almost turquoise in the fading light of the afternoon.

Her lips tingled, her nipples sharp little points straining against the cups of her sensible cotton bra. It seemed like every inch of her was waiting for what would happen next. And then there was a sudden fear that he might be the one to walk away first. He might be the sensible one. The one who could control whatever was driving them so recklessly now.

"Are you sure?" he said, his voice hoarse.

Three words, but they were ripe with meaning. The question for her was an important one. The fact that he'd pulled away to ask it, even more significant. The answer wasn't black and white, because she wasn't altogether sure. Of the fallout, anyway. But she was sure she wanted to take the risk. If there was *any* risk worth taking, it was with this man, in this moment.

She licked her lips, because she was still desperate for the taste of him. Then nodded. "I'm sure."

He watched her for a few seconds longer. Then, when he seemed satisfied she was thinking straight, or straight*ish*, he turned and picked something up. A plaid blanket. The blanket she sat on while keeping him company as he worked. She loved watching him work. His broad back to her, the thick muscles in his shoulders moving underneath his T-shirt. Sometimes he'd wear his baseball cap backward and his neck would be slick with sweat. She'd imagined more than once how it would feel to take that sweaty T-shirt off and move her hands up his hard, defined chest. And now...now that fantasy was within her reach. *He* was within reach. All six foot four, two hundred eighty pounds of him.

He walked around her and spread the blanket behind the plane where the straw was thickest. It was quiet in the old barn, with only soft sounds in the background—birds in the willow outside, the tinkling of the windchimes from the porch, the occasional swoosh of a truck passing on the highway. And the sound of the blood rushing in Savannah's ears.

She pushed her hair away from her face, watching Judd situate the blanket. Feeling the jagged little edges of her earring graze her palm. She wore the diamond studs her father had given her for her twelfth birthday, the exact age Maddie was now. He'd been the most important man in her life back then.

Judd turned and held out a hand.

When she looked at him she felt the sadness of her childhood ease from her shoulders. She felt joy seep into the cracks and crevices that had been left empty for so long. She saw someone that she wanted her son to be like. That *she* wanted to be like. A good person, a strong person.

She went to him, and slipped her hand in his. It fit there, almost perfectly, as he pulled her down on the blanket. Next to his big, warm body.

Savannah felt more alive than she had in years. Hyper aware of the straw that prickled her bare arm, of the thudding of Judd's heartbeat against her chest, of his breathing, steady and even over her temple.

She pulled in a breath, smelling his scent mixed with the hay, and closed her eyes as he cupped her cheek in his palm. The tips of his fingers were calloused and rough. He kissed one eyebrow, then the other, making his way down to her earlobe where the complicated diamond sparkled. He trailed his mouth down her neck, stopping at the hollow of her throat to touch it with his tongue.

She arched into him and wrapped her leg around the back of his thigh. He responded by pushing back, and she felt the sexy, masculine power of his body—the muscles that were coiled and hard, the long, taut tendons in his shoulders and arms. Every inch of him reminding her that what she was doing would only make her tumble faster, more out of control.

She bit her cheek as he began unbuttoning her blouse, and said a little prayer that he'd be gentle with her heart. That he wouldn't break her. That if he didn't end up wanting more, he'd be as kind as he was in every other aspect of his life, and would let her down easy.

He worked her blouse off, and then she lay there in just her bra and jeans.

"You are *so* beautiful," he whispered.

"You always say the sweetest things."

"But I'm not that sweet."

"I think you are," she said. "I think you're *very* sweet."

He slid his hand down her bare stomach and she shivered. Then worked his fingers into her jeans and underneath her panties.

She sucked in a breath at the brazenness of it, at the unapologetic boldness.

Smiling against her mouth, he nipped her bottom lip. "I'm really not."

"Okay. So you're not. I can live with that."

He unzipped her jeans, and she raised her bottom off the blanket so he could work them down her thighs. Then he peeled his T-shirt over his head and tossed it over a hay bale.

Naked from the waist up, he propped himself on one elbow and looked down at her. His broad, defined chest was sprinkled with the perfect amount of light brown hair which narrowed into a sexy line down his abs.

Mesmerized, she reached out and touched him. His nipples were small, caramel-colored points that hardened immediately underneath her fingertips.

She took him in, all of him. Her own body paled in comparison, and she wondered with a pang if he was finding her nearly as attractive.

As if in response, he cupped her cheek again and moved his thumb in a half arc under her eye. Then kissed her so deeply that he stole the air from her lungs. But if this was what drowning felt like, she welcomed it.

Reaching behind her, he unhooked her bra and pulled it off. Her nipples puckered in the evening air and he lowered his head. She shut her eyes as he closed his mouth around one, teasing the sensitive little bud with his tongue, nipping at it gently with his teeth, until she gasped and arched into him. Then he moved to the other one, licking, coaxing, until her entire breast ached for more.

And then he was moving lower, lower, kissing her stomach, her belly button. Then blowing lightly over the delicate elastic waistband of her underwear.

She gripped the blanket in both fists, quivering underneath his warm breath. She hadn't been touched like this in years, and only ever by Steven. Judd felt so different, his body heavy on hers, where Steven had been lighter. Hard where Steven had been soft. She'd always craved the intimacy after sex, the closeness more than the act itself. But now she wondered if she'd just been doing it wrong.

Judd pulled the crotch of her panties aside and trailed feathery kisses along her bikini line. Then pushed her knees apart, gently, gently...

She trembled from the inside out. Her eyes were still

screwed shut when she realized he was talking to her in low, raspy tones.

"Relax," he said. "You're okay."

She nodded, opening her eyes to see the rafters above, the dust particles floating in the gilded light. And then she felt his tongue flicking along her darkest folds, and she thought she might come undone.

Whimpering, she bit her lip to keep from crying out, even though nobody would hear if she did. It was the letting go, the giving in that she resisted the most.

And Judd sensed it.

He pushed her knees apart again, and buried his head between her legs. Exploring her, tasting her, and bringing her to the edge of something beautiful. And then she did cry out. She tumbled down, down, as her climax rose to meet her. She saw every color of the rainbow burst in a kaleidoscope behind her eyes. Firecrackers exploding, her stomach dropping as if she were on a roller coaster. Her toes curled and she arched her back, her body wracked with wave after wave of pleasure.

She felt his fingers press into her hips, felt his mouth move from the pulsing spot between her legs, over to her bikini line, where he tenderly repositioned her panties. He kissed her lower belly, and she gripped his shoulders in a desperate bid to keep him close.

He moved back up her body, the rough little hairs on his chest tickling her skin. His stubble scraped her neck, her cheek, in a complete contradiction to the softness of his lips.

He gathered her in his arms as she breathed the last heavy breaths of her orgasm.

She kissed his forearm, tasting his warm, salty skin, and reveled in the feeling that had overcome her completely.

"There's more where that came from," he said into her hair.

"But what about you?"

"Later. You're just starting to feel better. I don't want you to have a sex-induced setback."

She laughed. "I wonder how many emergency room visits they see from multiple orgasms."

"Not nearly enough."

Shifting in his arms, she kissed him on the jaw. "I want you to…" She didn't know how to say it without heat flooding her cheeks. This was a first for her. In a long line of firsts.

"What?"

She cleared her throat, emboldened by how his hand cupped her backside. So easily. So possessive, like she was his. "I don't want to be done yet."

He raised his sandy brows, but stayed completely still.

She reached down and cupped the rock-hard bulge in his jeans, surprising herself.

"What exactly do you have in mind?" he asked, his voice gravelly.

She pushed at his shoulders until he was on his back looking up at her.

Reaching down to unbuckle his belt, she pulled in a breath.

"Savannah…"

"Hmm?"

"I don't have a condom, baby. This might have to wait."

She loved that he'd just said that. Loved that he was responsible and mature. And she wanted him more than ever.

"I've been on the pill since Wyatt," she said. "I'm okay with no condom if you are. I trust you." And she meant it.

He watched as she worked his jeans down, then his stark-white jockeys. His erection sprang free and she gaped at it for a minute. *Huge.* Just like the rest of him…

Wet and aching, she wriggled out of her underwear, and straddled him. Wrapping a hand around his shaft, she settled herself down and guided him where she wanted him most.

He closed his eyes for a second, his body going rigid. Then, he grabbed her butt with both hands, his biceps bunching and flexing as he lifted his hips and buried himself inside her.

"Jesus," he breathed.

She planted her hands on his thick shoulders, and rocked forward. He felt so, so good. He moved with her, their bodies finding a searing, instinctive rhythm. She felt her hair swing against her shoulder blades, felt it graze her lower back. Her breasts jiggled, her nipples jutting into the air, and he reached up to cup them as her second orgasm mounted like a slow wave.

She gripped him with her thighs and threw her head back as a feeling of pure, physical rapture crested and then rippled in hot currents through her body. Then rippled through his. She felt his hands slide up her arms, his callouses scratching her skin, as he sought to hold her steady.

But it was too late. She'd already fallen. Just like she'd known she would.

Chapter Seventeen

S AVANNAH LOOKED AROUND the small bedroom that she'd been sharing with Wyatt for the past week, and fought a familiar ache in her throat.

Swallowing it down, she picked up her robe from the back of the chair by the window, and stuffed it into her bag. It was the last of her things. She'd packed Wyatt's an hour ago.

The early morning sun shone through the sheer, butter-colored curtains, and gleamed over the hardwood floor. As usual, the house smelled of coffee and breakfast—what had become a tradition since they'd come to stay. It didn't matter that this was her first day back at work since Wyatt's surgery, and it was so early even the goats hadn't sauntered into the pasture yet. Judd had still woken up before everyone else, and had made them something to eat.

She stood with her hands on her hips, feeling strange in her knee-length pencil skirt and silky blouse after so many days in soft, frayed jeans and T-shirts. Her heart felt strange, too. As if it no longer fit comfortably inside her chest. It was swollen and tender, and she couldn't decide whether what happened with Judd was a huge mistake, or the best thing she'd ever done.

They hadn't had time to talk since last night. Tanner had brought Maddie and Wyatt back as the sun was going down, and Savannah had headed inside to make dinner, still floating around on a euphoric cloud.

They'd spent the rest of the evening on the couch watching a movie, but of course everything between them felt fundamentally different. More significant, more delicate.

Whatever relationship they might have after this, or might *not* have, Savannah knew she couldn't stay forever. She had to get Wyatt back to his normal routine. And she had to get back to hers, too. The longer they stayed at the farm, the more neither one wanted to go home to their little bungalow in town.

She turned at the sound of Wyatt's laughter from the kitchen. Of course, he'd still be here with Maddie during the day, so at least he wouldn't feel too severed from what he'd grown used to this past week. Savannah on the other hand…

Sighing, she walked over to where her purse hung on the back of the door. She reached for the strap just as her phone rang from the side pocket.

Digging it out, her heart slowed when she saw Steven's number. He'd been calling and she hadn't called him back yet, relying on texts to communicate since Wyatt's surgery. She felt a pang of guilt thinking about sending him to voicemail again.

She steeled herself and hit the little green button.

"Hello?"

"Savannah," he said. "How are you?"

She walked back to the other side of the room, her heels tapping hollowly on the wood floor, and opened the curtains. Partly because she loved the view. Partly because she didn't really want Wyatt hearing this conversation. Or Judd for that matter.

"I'm doing well," she said. "I've been meaning to call you back…"

"Yeah, I was wondering if you were still alive." There was a smile in his voice. He'd always been good-natured. A total flop in the husband and father department, but good-natured nonetheless. "How's our little man?"

She stiffened at that. It seemed so easy for him now. Where had he been last year when Wyatt was getting teased about his lip at daycare, or when she'd had trouble paying the electric bill?

"He's fine, Steven," she said evenly. "You know, I might have to call you back. I'm getting ready for work. I've been gone so many days, and I don't want to be late…"

"Oh, yeah. Yeah, that's no problem. I know you're busy."

Switching the phone to her other ear, she heard footsteps coming down the hallway. Her cheeks heated. Steven was Wyatt's dad. There wasn't anything wrong with talking to him this morning. The morning after she'd just had sex with Judd… *Ugh.* There really wasn't anything wrong with it, but it felt gross anyway. Especially since she knew what this call was all about. Steven wanted to come visit. And she had a feeling from how persistent he'd been, there might be something more to it.

She ran her tongue along her top lip, tasting her lipstick. It felt just as out of place as her skirt and pumps did. Suddenly, she longed for the art studio, and its familiar walls, the bright, hot fire in the oven. The way she could always lose herself in the beauty of the glass.

"It's just that I was wondering…" He cleared his throat. "I was wondering if I could come see Wyatt this weekend. And you. If I could come see you both."

She sat heavily on the bed, but caught herself before she sighed into the phone.

"I know it's a lot to ask," he continued. "And you might not be happy to see me. I guess that's an understatement. Wyatt doesn't even know me."

There was a legitimately miserable tone to his voice that made her sad. Then she reminded herself that he'd been the one to leave. And nobody, especially not Savannah, had stopped him from coming back. This wasn't her fault. It wasn't Wyatt's fault. It was Steven's fault.

But she simply couldn't ignore the fact that he was trying. She knew he was holding down a job, had an apartment, was sending the periodic check now. It was a start. Gran would say it was too little, too late, but it was something. After he'd left, Savannah had always hoped for something. And here it was.

Only now, it just didn't feel as significant as she'd imagined.

She reached out and touched the delicate curtains, marveling at how someone so big and tough as Judd would pick something so pretty for this room. But Judd was an anomaly.

Pulling in a breath, she ignored the tightening of her stomach, the weird, conflicted feeling in her heart, and said what she knew was the right thing. The right thing for Wyatt. If not for her.

"You can come see us, Steven," she said. "Wyatt would love that."

⟫⟫⟫✗⟪⟪⟪

JUDD STOOD OUTSIDE the bedroom door, poised to knock. But the walls were thin, and there was a gap between the door and the floorboards, and he'd heard part of Savannah's conversation before he could help himself.

Part of it. Not all of it. But enough that he lowered his fist now and let it drop to his side. *Wyatt would love that...*

It didn't take a rocket scientist to figure out the infamous Steven was coming back to town.

A few weeks ago, Judd would've been hard pressed to admit that bothering him. But after last night, after cupping Savannah's breasts while she climaxed... Well, now it bothered him. A lot.

What the fuck was he going to do about it?

He stepped carefully away from the door, then walked into the living room with his hands laced behind his head.

So Steven was coming back. At least temporarily. Judd gritted his teeth and stared out the window to the barn. Frank waddled around his truck pecking at bugs. The goats had made their appearance and grazed as one indiscriminate brown and white blob next to the fence. The farm was just

159

waking up—peaceful, quiet. But inside the house, Judd felt dangerously close to cracking in half.

Taking a deep breath, he lowered his hands and put them in his pockets. He was jealous, which was an emotion he detested. He was also irritated with himself. What the hell did he think was going to happen? Savannah had an ex who'd most likely be involved in his son's life in one way or another. And seeing her would go with the territory.

Judd frowned at the sun making its way over the barn roof. Cheerful, bright. Giving him and his bad attitude one big golden finger. Despite how it felt having Savannah and Wyatt stay with him for a week, that didn't make them his family. Again, he reminded himself he wasn't ready for a family. He wasn't ready for commitment. He wasn't ready to fall in love.

His jaw muscles bunched. Was that what he was doing? Was he falling in love? Or maybe he was already in love, and it had snuck up on him like some kind of brick to the side of the head. Or heart. He didn't even know anymore.

All he knew was that he was going to have to deal with this emotion ramming its way through him. He'd just need to get used to someone else being in Savannah and Wyatt's life. Someone who had every right to be there, despite some pretty shitty-ass choices in the beginning. This wasn't Judd's rodeo. It was Steven Casteele's.

From the kitchen, he heard Wyatt knocking on the window trying to get Darryl and Darryl's attention. He smiled when the goats looked up, grass sticking out the sides of their mouths. They took a few steps toward the house, like they wanted the kids to come out and play. Or bring snacks. Either, or.

Judd crossed his arms over his chest, his smile fading. It *was* another man's rodeo. But that didn't mean Judd didn't have a stake in it.

A fairly big stake, by the feel of it.

Chapter Eighteen

J UDD'S TRUCK RUMBLED its way down the long highway that led into town. Savannah had left her car at her place, so he was going to drop her off, and she'd go to work from there. Wyatt had stayed at the farm with Maddie, both of them standing on the front porch steps waving goodbye in the early morning sunlight.

The cab was quiet except for the low sound of country music coming from the speakers. Every now and then she'd sneak a look in Judd's direction, but he kept staring straight ahead, his jaw working underneath his thick, morning stubble. His big hand lay casually on her thigh, though. A reminder that they'd officially moved out of the friend zone and into somewhere else entirely.

Breathing in his clean scent, she wrapped her fingers around his, and rubbed her thumb over the backs of his knuckles.

He glanced over, letting his gaze fall to her skirt that was riding up over her knees. She thought it was pretty conservative, except for the fit, which was snug. But he knew exactly what she looked like underneath, and that made her ears burn.

He didn't smile. Didn't say anything. Just looked at her in that dark, hungry way of his, and then let his gaze settle back on the road.

She watched him, feeling something between them this morning that didn't have anything to do with the sex yesterday. She thought of the phone call with Steven, and the footsteps she'd heard in the hallway.

Squeezing his hand, she shifted underneath her seat belt to face him better. "Is anything wrong?"

He didn't look over. "Why would you think that?"

"You're just quiet. Quieter than usual."

"Just thinking."

"About?"

He rubbed his thumb over the steering wheel, looking pensive. "My aunt Vivian wants to fly in, for one. She emailed this morning."

"Oh… You don't want her to come?"

"No, she's great. But she judges, I think without meaning to. We always feel like we're under a microscope when she's here. Wondering if we're doing the right thing by Maddie, screwing her up. That kind of thing."

"There's no way anyone could think you were screwing her up," Savannah said. "She's so happy."

"She is. But happiness is only part of it. Sometimes I worry she doesn't have a stable enough home life. She bounces around between Tanner and Luke and me every day of the week."

"Judd, she doesn't bounce around. She has a home base with Tanner, and she gets to choose between you three.

That's the best of all worlds. She loves it."

"I hope so. But it's not the kind of family we wanted for her."

"Families don't have to be traditional to be loving and secure."

He looked over, his expression softening. She could've been talking about her situation with Wyatt.

"No. You're right," he said. "They don't."

They rode in silence for another minute, and Savannah put her shade down against the sun's glare.

"What else?" she finally asked.

"Mmm?"

"You said that Vivian wanting to fly in was the first thing. What's the second?"

He stayed quiet, staring straight ahead.

"Judd."

"Yeah."

"You can talk to me, you know."

They were passing more houses now, more cars as people headed out for their day. She didn't want to be going back to work. She wanted to stay with Judd. Get naked and burrow underneath his covers all afternoon. She tried pushing down the thought that he'd be going back to work soon, too. What they'd shared this last week was going to change. In one form or another, it would have to.

He sighed, and took his hand away to rest it on his thigh. "It's nothing huge. Just figuring out how to feel about your ex-husband coming back, that's all."

Savannah's chest constricted. So he *had* heard. She didn't

know where to start. This was such new, bumpy territory that her tongue sat wedged between her teeth.

He glanced over. "I heard you on the phone this morning. I was going to tell you breakfast was ready. Sorry."

"No...no, don't be sorry."

"Eavesdropping isn't my thing. Neither is controlling what women do. So don't worry about that part, okay?"

Her eyes burned. It wasn't that she wanted him to feel possessive of her. It wasn't that. But maybe she was hoping he'd want to lay a little claim. Just a little one...

He didn't sound mad. He didn't sound...anything, really. He sounded detached, and that hurt more than she was prepared for.

She watched him. Of course, it was possible he was just protecting himself, and she could understand that. If he had an ex-wife who was getting ready to visit, she'd be protecting herself, too. Probably in the form of slamming the door in his face.

"Just so you know," she said, "he's coming to see Wyatt."

He looked over, his lips tilting maddeningly.

"What?"

"Savannah..."

"What?"

"Don't be naïve."

"I'm not being naïve."

"You are if you think he's not wanting you back."

She stiffened and looked out the window, watching the historic brick buildings of town come into view. "Maybe," she said. "But Steven had his chance."

"You don't feel like giving him another one?"

She glanced over, but she couldn't tell what the hell he was thinking. She remembered what he'd said about his mother, and wondered if he was drawing a comparison now. Maybe she never really stood a chance with Judd. She was damned if she did, damned if she didn't. Give someone a second chance, and be a doormat. Stand her ground, and be alone for the rest of her life.

"Don't answer that," he said. "It's none of my business."

She felt her mouth hang open. "Well, it's a *little* of your business, don't you think?"

"You need to take me out of the equation and do what's best for you and Wyatt."

"So you *do* think I'd take him back."

"I didn't say that."

"What are you saying, Judd? Because I'm having a hard time reading you right now."

"That's probably because I'm trying really fucking hard to do the right thing, and give you the space and respect you deserve as someone in charge of her own life."

"And pushing me away while you're at it."

"I'm not pushing you away."

She crossed her arms over her chest.

He slid her a look. "Okay. Maybe I'm pushing you away a little. But not because I want to, believe me."

Slowing the truck, he turned down her street.

The hardest part was, she recognized the hypocrisy, because she was the queen of pushing people away. She understood where Judd was coming from, because that's where she permanently resided these days.

She reached for her purse as he pulled up to her bunga-low. It looked smaller than when they'd left it last week. When she'd been in the throes of the worst fever of her adult life. When he'd appeared and had taken care of her and her son when she'd needed him most. She'd always love him for that. No matter how far away he tried to push her. And how hard she pushed back.

He put the big truck in park and turned, his eyes impos-sibly blue in the morning light. "I really am trying to be a decent guy here."

She smiled, wanting to reach up and touch his face. But worried if she did, she wouldn't leave. She was already having trouble tearing her gaze away from his lips. "I know you are. But you know what else you are, Judd Harlow?"

"What."

"A heartbreaker," she said. Then leaned over and kissed him on the side of the mouth.

Before he could reach for her hand, she'd scooted over and opened the heavy door. She hopped out, surprisingly nimble on the heels, and turned around to look at him.

He was leaning over the seat toward her, taking up so much of the cab, she wondered how she'd fit next to him in the first place.

"Take care," he said.

She should've expected that. A no-frills goodbye. For now, at least. No fuss, no drama. He'd meant exactly what he'd said before—he was going to try and give her the space she'd said she'd wanted. Only now, that space didn't feel so wise, as it felt lonely.

Swallowing, she nodded and closed the door. *One thing at a time.* She just needed to get through this weekend. She'd deal with Steven and start laying some sort of foundation they could build on for Wyatt's sake. So they could parent him together, not apart, like he deserved.

And she'd try doing it without thinking of someone else the entire time.

Chapter Nineteen

S AVANNAH WALKED QUIETLY beside Steven, while Wyatt ran up ahead. This was the first Saturday of Marietta's Movies Under the Stars, where the entire town was invited to the park next to St. James Church, to watch classics from the eighties projected onto a giant screen. The grassy hill made for a perfect outdoor theater underneath the soft, velvety sky, and the distant laughter of kids and families promised a fun night.

Except Savannah couldn't stop wishing she was there with Judd instead. As Steven chatted amiably next to her, even reaching out at one point to guide her away from a hole in the sidewalk, it was feeling too much like a date for comfort.

He looked over at her now and smiled. He was just starting to relax, after spending the first hour at her house apologizing for everything he'd ever done in his life. He felt genuinely awful, that was obvious. It was also obvious he wanted another chance. Definitely with Wyatt. Possibly with her, although he hadn't said as much.

She smiled back. He looked good—handsome in a preppy kind of way, and fit. He'd lost the baby fat he'd carried around since high school, and was now running regularly. It showed.

He'd matured in his years away from Marietta. There was a wizened edge to his eyes. As well as a look of regret that aged him. Overall, her high school sweetheart had grown into a nice-looking man, shedding a good portion of the selfishness that had dictated his every move in his early twenties. Which was great. It really was. But there was no way she was going back to the way they'd been. Too much water had passed under that bridge, weakening it beyond repair.

As much as Savannah longed for a family again, this wasn't the way. In a few days, she'd make that clear. But for now, she wanted Wyatt to have this time with his dad to start fresh. New.

"That looks like a good place over there," Steven said, pointing to a spot underneath a leafy maple. There were a lot of people there already, and the sun wouldn't go down for another half hour or so.

Savannah nodded and took out the quilt that Gran had made right after Wyatt turned two. It was a patchwork of all his old onesies, and was her favorite thing in the world.

She leaned down to make sure the grass wasn't wet before spreading the blanket out.

Steven set the picnic basket down, which consisted mostly of Goldfish and juice boxes, and waited for Savannah to sit before he settled in beside her. She caught the scent of his aftershave. Something sweeter, stronger than Judd wore, and her stomach dropped. It had only been a few days, but she missed him so much that her eyes stung, and she had to look away before they filled with tears.

"Anything wrong?"

She forced a smile, smoothing her skirt over her lap. "Nope. Just thinking."

"Mama?" Wyatt plopped down on the edge of the blanket, careful not to get his shoes on it. His lip was healing well, and he looked so cute in his little collared shirt. Such a good, sweet boy. And right now, he was thriving. The surgery, the time at the farm with Maddie and Judd, the promise of a long, full summer ahead. It was all so good for him, that she felt an overwhelming sense of gratitude.

"What, baby?"

"I see Maddie. Can I go say hi?"

Savannah's heart skipped a beat. "She's here? Where?"

"Over there," he said, pointing down the hill.

Savannah craned her neck and saw Maddie who was standing near the screen with some girls her age. But she didn't see Tanner or Luke. Or Judd. Maybe he'd dropped her off. She was old enough to do something like this by herself. But Savannah still couldn't help looking for him. Hoping she'd see him. Praying she wouldn't. Not with Steven sitting so close.

"Okay, baby. But stay where I can see you, okay? No running off."

"Okay, Mom."

Steven looked over. "Want me to go with him?"

"No, he's all right. He knows not to go far."

It was such a small thing. But Steven didn't even know

enough about his son to trust him with something like this. It was a reminder of how much he'd missed out on. Of how much time he had to make up.

They watched Wyatt bound down the hill. Watched him call out to Maddie, and her bend to sweep him up. After a second, he pointed to where Savannah and Steven were sitting on the blanket, and Maddie waved.

"Who's that?" Steven asked, shielding his eyes from the sun.

"His babysitter. She's wonderful."

"She's tall."

"You should see her brothers."

Maybe the tone of her voice had changed slightly, warmed because she was picturing Judd. But Steven's gaze shifted back then, taking her in. The look in his eyes was unmistakable, and she flushed.

"You look beautiful tonight," he said. "But you always were."

She picked at a thread on her skirt, as the evening breeze stroked her bare shoulders. "Thanks, Steven."

"I probably don't have any right to say that. Or maybe you don't want to hear it."

"It's always nice to hear."

"Even from me?"

Her lips tilted. "Even from you."

They sat in silence for a minute, kids running back and forth in front of their blanket. Someone was cooking hot dogs on a little hibachi grill nearby, and it smelled like summertime. Her stomach growled.

Steven stretched his legs in front of him, and turned toward her, leaning on one elbow. His skin was smooth and tan, his hair that sun-kissed blond that had always made her swoony at nineteen. He was clean-shaven, his jaw hard and angular in the early evening light.

"Do you ever wonder what it might've been like for us?" he asked quietly.

She pulled on the thread again, stopping herself before she'd made a hole in the fabric. "What it would've been like...if you hadn't left?"

He nodded. The question was all encompassing. Impossible to answer in just one sentence, or just one evening, or just one lifetime. She'd wondered, and she'd cried, and she'd cursed him more times than she could count. But that part of her life was over. Steven wasn't the only one who'd grown. Savannah had grown, too. She'd grown wiser, and more aware of the world around her. More aware of what could hurt her, and how she could move on after the worst pain she'd ever experienced. It wasn't so much a question that she couldn't answer, as a question she didn't want to answer.

"I've thought about it," he said.

How many times had she imagined this moment? When he'd finally realized what he'd done, and asked her to reconsider with his heart on his sleeve.

"I was so stupid for leaving you, Savannah," Steven said. "I was so stupid for leaving our son. But I was scared of the kind of dad I'd turn out to be. And at the time..." He paused, his eyes bright. "At the time leaving was easier than failing."

She stared at him. "But you left knowing that's what my own dad did. How I never really got over that. Wyatt would've loved you through your mistakes. You didn't trust him enough to give him the chance."

He put his hand on her thigh. Its weight felt familiar and wrong at the same time. They'd grown up together. Made a child together. Had been friends before they'd been lovers. But her adult heart had finally escaped the chains that he'd wrapped around it all those years ago.

"Would you have loved me through my mistakes, too?" he asked.

She looked down at his hand. How tan the skin was. How thick, masculine veins snaked over the knuckles. At one time they'd been as familiar on her body as her own. At one time, she would've done anything for Steven, gone anywhere he'd asked her to. But she wasn't that girl anymore.

She put her hand over his. "I would have," she said. "And I did."

He watched her, his lips parted slightly. Waiting.

"I'll always love you, Steven," she said. "But I don't love you like you want me to. Not anymore."

"I'm not the same guy I was before. I've changed. I've grown."

She squeezed his fingers, the memories thick behind her eyes. Wearing his letterman's jacket, and how safe she'd felt with it draped over her shoulders. She'd known he'd never leave her. He'd never let her down. How wrong she'd been…

"I know you have," she said. "And I have, too. We've

grown. But we've also grown apart. After all this time? It was always going to end up this way."

"It doesn't have to be like that. We could be a family again. We could take it slow, as slow as you wanted."

"Steven—"

He leaned closer. His eyes were so clear that she could see herself in them. But not her teenage self. This was the image of a woman who'd been hurt, who'd been financially strained, emotionally gutted. A woman who'd cried herself to sleep so many times, she couldn't keep track anymore.

"Don't answer now," he said, his voice low. "Just think about it. Please."

"Mama!"

She turned to see Wyatt scrambling up the grassy hill.

"Judd says Frank laid eggs! Frank's a girl, Mama!"

She laughed. "What?"

And then Judd appeared, walking behind her son like a cowboy in a western. Sexy, broad-shouldered, swaggering Judd.

Her heart curled around itself at the sight of him, of his worn Levi's and plaid shirt open at the throat. At the way he was turning every female head within a fifty-foot radius. At how he had eyes only for her.

They took her in. All of her. All of Steven, too. And they cooled.

It was only then that she realized Steven's hand was still on her thigh. Her face burned.

Steven smiled. He knew Judd was a family friend who'd flown them to and from Chicago. Savannah hadn't told him anything else, so it was only Judd who wore the slightly stony expression.

Wyatt flopped down on the blanket, and Steven got up, holding out his hand.

"Hey, man. Steven Casteele."

Judd nodded, shaking it. His gaze shifted to Savannah, then back again.

"Nice to meet you," he said.

"Judd, right?"

"That's right."

Steven put his hands in his pockets. He wasn't short, but he had to look up at Judd to make conversation. "Savannah told me about you flying them back and forth for Wyatt's surgery. That was very cool."

"I was happy to do it." This without looking at Savannah again. The expression on his face was detached, distant. Not unfriendly, just so unlike what she'd come to expect over the past few weeks. More like how he'd acted that first day in the hangar.

The sun had gone down, and the evening air was cool. A flock of starlings flew overhead in a dark, fluid cloud. Families began settling in on their blankets, sipping warm drinks from thermoses.

An awkward silence settled over them. Finally, Judd nodded to a spot down the hill. "I'd better get back to Maddie. Good to meet you, man."

He looked briefly at Savannah, then turned and walked away.

Steven sat back down, watching him go. "Now, that's a

guy who doesn't have a lot to say."

That's what most people would think. That's what she'd thought herself. But Judd just leaned toward quality instead of quantity. There weren't a ton of words, but he never wasted them. They always packed a punch.

Pulling her knees up to her chest, she hugged them. She watched him head down the hill, his big frame growing shadowy in the distance. She longed to get up and follow him. To ask if there was room on their blanket for her and Wyatt. To watch the movie with his arm around her, keeping her warm.

"He's just quiet," she said.

Steven glanced over as Wyatt dug in the picnic basket for his crackers. "You know him pretty well?"

She nodded.

"How well?"

She slid him a look.

"I know," he said. "None of my business."

They were quiet for a minute as the parks and recreation employees began setting up the projector. A couple of kids with sparklers chased each other a few yards away.

"I just want you to be happy, Savannah," Steven finally said. His voice was soft. Almost resigned. "You deserve it."

She turned and gave him a faint smile. She did love him. A part of her always would, no matter how badly things had gone between them. He was the father of her child.

"I am happy," she said.

And meant it.

Chapter Twenty

JUDD PULLED AWAY from Luke's place, with Maddie and Scooter in the window. The dog was licking her ear, while she waved with the TV on in the background.

She'd wanted to spend the night after the movie. Luke lived close to the dog park, and going on Sunday mornings was a new Luke/Maddie tradition. They got up early, picked up Mary, got donuts, and took Scooter to his play dates. It was like dog church. And it was ridiculous.

Smiling, he waved back. But by the time he got to the stop sign on Third Street, his mood was heavy again. He'd been pushing Savannah to the back of his mind all night, but she refused to stay put. He kept picturing her sitting on that blanket looking down at her ex-husband, her eyes hooded, her lips plump. And they'd been holding hands. He'd zeroed in on that part right away.

His gut tightened at the memory. No matter how hard he tried to rationalize it, there was no use. He felt the way he felt. Like he wanted to unzip his skin and step right out of it.

He sat at the stop sign, his blinker flashing through the darkness. People were still making their way home from the park in a steady stream. She'd probably be back to her place by now. Maybe with Steven.

Judd didn't chase after women. He never had before and he sure as hell wasn't about to start now. But he *did* have to get home. And if he drove by her house on the way…well, then. It wasn't chasing. It was taking the scenic route.

Before he could talk himself out of it, he turned left instead of right, and headed down the wide, dark street. The moon was only a sliver tonight, the stars twinkling like diamonds in the sky.

He narrowed his eyes at someone walking ahead. A woman, slender, long skirt, shapely backside. Familiar.

Slowing the truck, he leaned forward. It was her. He recognized the tilt of her head, the way she hugged herself, like she was cold.

He pulled over and rolled down the window. "Savannah?"

She turned. God, she was gorgeous. She smiled, her skin milky and smooth underneath the almost erotic light of the streetlamp.

"What are you doing?" he asked. "Where's Wyatt?"

She made her way toward the truck. "Steven wanted to take him for ice cream after the movie. I thought it would be good for them to have some time together. And a walk home sounded nice."

He watched her steadily.

She licked her lips, looking shy all of a sudden. "But seeing you is nicer."

His dick reacted immediately. She hadn't meant that in a sexual way, but it didn't matter. Everything about her was sexual at the moment. Then he remembered how she'd looked at Steven earlier, and he swallowed hard.

"You want a ride?"

"I'd love one."

She walked around the truck and climbed in. He immediately caught her scent and it did things to him that felt primal and raw.

She settled in and tugged the seat belt across her chest. He looked over, let his gaze fall to the soft swell of her breasts underneath the sweater, then looked back at the road.

The truck sat there idling, and he opened his mouth to say something, then closed it again. He could feel her watching him.

"You surprised me tonight," she said. "I didn't know you'd be there."

"It showed." *Goddamn it.* He hadn't meant to say a damn thing. He wished he could suck the words back in, but it was too late. They hung there, bitter and accusatory.

"What's that supposed to mean?" she asked.

"Nothing."

He shifted into first, but she reached out to stop him.

"Judd. What'd you mean by that?"

"What do you think I meant?"

Jesus. What a prick. If he wasn't careful, he'd alienate her completely. And maybe deep down, that's what he was going for. If she was pissed, it was a hell of a lot harder to get close.

It worked. Leaning back, she glared at him.

"I assume you're referring to Steven?"

"Maybe."

"Didn't you make a big speech the other night about how I shouldn't throw you into the mix?"

"Something like that."

"And now you're doing a one-eighty," she said. "Also, not that it matters, but it wasn't what it looked like."

He laughed. "Okay."

"Well, excuse me. I didn't think you cared that much."

"I care. And seeing his hand on your thigh makes me care even more." *Shit. That didn't come out right.*

"So, now you're just being a jerk," she said. "You don't give a damn about me, you just want to control what I do?"

"No."

"Then what?"

He shifted in his seat. She was right. Absolutely, one-hundred percent right. He wanted his cake and wanted to eat it, too. He wanted Savannah for himself, but he didn't want to commit, either. Did he?

Heat crept up his neck. Now he was pissed, too. This wasn't going to end well.

"What do you want from me, Judd?" she asked. "Be honest."

"I don't want his hand on your thigh anymore."

She rolled her eyes. "That's all you've got? For your information, I didn't really want it there, either. I wanted *yours* there. But I have some stuff I need to work out with Steven. That's just a fact."

"I know. I know you do. But it's how I feel."

After a long minute, she unhooked her seat belt and scooted toward him. Not too close. But close enough.

"I feel the same way," she said. "But it's complicated."

"What's complicated about it? Either we're seeing each other, or we're not."

Cars passed them on the street, their headlights flashing into the cab of the truck, before leaving it dim again.

"God, I want that more than anything," she said. "But I can't just casually hook up right now. I can't. I'm gonna end up with a broken heart. I can see it on your face, the hesitation. And it kills me."

"I don't have anything written on my face."

"Really."

"And who said anything about casually hooking up?"

"Well, what am I supposed to think? Marriage?"

He watched her. The way her eyelashes cast a dark shadow over her cheek. The way her pupils had swallowed the green of her irises whole. All he could fathom at that moment was *her*. How much he wanted her. How much he wanted all of her, every single bit she was willing to give.

"Why not?" he said.

And like with every other thing that had escaped his mouth in the past five minutes, it was out before he could process exactly what it was he'd said. What it really meant.

His heart hammered in his chest, and she stared at him.

"What?"

"I want to be with you," he said.

"But...you don't want to *marry* me. That's ridiculous. It's too fast."

He stared back, his jaw working. Judd didn't like to be told what was possible and what wasn't. He never had. His heartbeat slowed a fraction and he took an even breath.

"Don't tell me it's ridiculous. Fast, yeah. But not ridiculous."

She laughed again, sounding almost loopy. "You don't mean this. You're mad and trying to make a point. I'm not going to pretend it's real, because it's not."

"Goddamn it, Savannah," he growled. "I *love* you."

"And I love *you.*"

They scowled at each other through the darkness. Maybe neither one of them realized just what the hell they were saying. He wanted to reach out and pull her to him, to be done with this conversation and how it was making him feel. Cracked wide open. But he was too stunned to do anything but sit there and listen to the sound of his own shallow breathing.

He'd actually brought up *marriage.* Him. Of all people. The guy who thought happy marriages, truly happy marriages, weren't really possible. And yet, here he was. Sickened at the thought of letting this one get away. Hoping that maybe he'd been wrong all these years. That maybe relationships could last if they were nurtured lovingly enough.

After a long, pregnant minute, she scooted back and leaned against the door. She watched him like he was some kind of predator who'd snatch her up as soon as she wasn't looking.

"Don't you understand?" she said, her voice wavering. "This is what I've always wanted. Ever since I was a little girl. Ever since my dad left. I've wanted a family of my own. And it took a really long time to be okay with it being just me and

Wyatt. And now…" Her eyes were glassy. He could see how bright they were even through the minimal light in the truck. "Here you are, offering me everything. And I can't help but think to you, it's just a what-if type question. But to me…"

"Savannah…"

He reached for her hand, but she pulled away.

"Don't do this to me, Judd. What happens when you wake up tomorrow and want to take it back? If you truly love me, you won't mention it again."

He stared at her, his hands heavy, his heart lumbering inside his chest. "You don't trust me."

"Would you?" she said. "If you were me?"

He had no idea what just happened. Had he proposed? Had he actually been serious? Or was she right—had it been one big what-if?

He needed to think. To process this. Decide where she fit into his life, and how he was going to come to terms with how tonight had nearly run him over. Like a train hurdling down the tracks with nobody at the controls.

"Tell me I didn't just lose you," she said, tears welling in her eyes. "Because it feels like something happened just now. Did something happen between us?"

None of this was her fault. He couldn't blame her, as much as he could blame a snowball for causing an avalanche. The truth was, all this had been simmering inside him for a long time. Since he'd been a kid, really. His understanding of relationships, of true commitment, was so fucked up.

Savannah was just protecting herself, being shrewd, wary. Exactly how she should be. That's usually how he was, too.

But tonight, his walls had fallen away for some inexplicable reason, exposing his heart in its most vulnerable form. And she'd turned him away, because she didn't trust him. Because he hadn't given her enough time to get to *know* him. Like an idiot.

But knowing why didn't make it any easier. Because the boy in him was overriding the man. The hurt overpowering the rationale. And suddenly, all he wanted was to be in his plane, flying somewhere. Where he'd always felt the most in control. Where he could think without complication.

Wrapping his fist around the gear shift, he squeezed harder than he meant. He looked straight ahead at the little street, lined with maples and cute houses with warm yellow light spilling from their windows. So many people inside those houses, with so many different kinds of lives. Single people, couples, families. Some were happy. Some weren't. And for a second, he let himself picture the ramshackle cottage he'd grown up in. How he'd vowed things would be different when he got older. For him, and his brothers and sister. How he'd never let anyone hurt them again. They'd always be together. Always.

Up until now he'd done a pretty good job of fulfilling that vow. They'd remained close. They'd avoided more pain. They were a family, for better or worse. But a family with walls. The question was, when was he going to lower his for good and allow some happiness in?

"Yeah," he said, his voice husky. "Something happened between us, Savannah."

He could hear her breathing—the quick breaths of

someone who was trying to stop crying. And he could feel her gaze on him, tearing at his resolve.

"Now I just need to figure out what it all means," he continued. "Before I screw us both up."

Chapter Twenty-One

S AVANNAH SPENT THE rest of the night pacing the floor. After Steven had brought Wyatt home, she'd thanked him for visiting, and he'd kissed her on the cheek. She'd remained kind, but her body turned stiff the second his lips made contact, and he'd finally pulled away from her house looking subdued.

She stood at the window now though, glad he'd come. Glad they were on their way to repairing a relationship for Wyatt. And glad she'd ended up telling him exactly where they stood. That there was no way they were getting back together. Now, or ever. And in order for them to move on in a healthy way, he had to accept that.

Shifting on her feet, she resisted the urge to check her cell again. She'd been thinking about Judd nonstop. Going over and over what he'd said in his truck. And when she'd put Wyatt to bed, kissing his downy head, she found herself choking up all over again.

It was funny, how only a few short years ago, she would've processed those words of his differently. She would have heard in them what she wanted to hear, and discarded the rest. But now she wanted more. She believed she deserved more. And so did Wyatt. Being with Judd wasn't enough. She wanted his heart, but she coveted his devotion, too. A what-if scenario wasn't enough to build a life on. And she wanted a life with him more than anything.

But the way he'd looked when she'd gotten out of his truck scared her. She knew he was going to retreat back inside himself, and there might be no recovering from that.

He'd left without kissing her goodbye, without telling her they'd see each other soon. And the finality of that was killing her where she stood.

The sky flickered in the distance. The stars that had twinkled over the park earlier were now snuffed out by storm clouds. She could smell the impending rain in the air, felt the electricity.

Rubbing her arms, she looked over at the clock on the wall. Almost dawn. She'd been up all night. But it had felt more like three nights, stretching on and on and on.

She stared back out the window to the shadowy trees in her yard. She'd wait a few more hours, and then she was calling him. They needed to talk. He'd said he'd wanted to figure things out.

But they needed to figure things out together.

SAVANNAH RUFFLED WYATT'S hair. He was in the middle of his second bowl of Rice Krispies, and she pointed to the orange slices beside his bowl.

"No more until those are gone, buddy."

"Okay, Mama."

She reached for her phone. It was almost eight.

Outside, the wind had picked up and sharp little raindrops were pelting the kitchen window. The weather guy had said the storm was going to miss Marietta and they'd only get the residual nastiness, but the clouds gathering overhead suggested otherwise.

Frowning, Savannah headed into the dim living room and turned on a lamp.

She dialed Judd's number, sat heavily on the couch, and waited. When his voicemail kicked on, her heart sank. Maybe he was going to ignore her. Refuse to take her calls.

At the thought, she stiffened. If he was planning on running the other way, she'd already decided watching him go wasn't an option. At least not without a fight. She didn't want to casually hook up. But she didn't want it to end, either. She was holding out hope that she could put her fears aside long enough to give whatever was happening between them a chance. And that he'd be able to do the same.

She sent a quick text. Telling him she loved him. Telling him she wanted to talk. And waited.

An hour turned into two, and she still hadn't heard back when thunder began rumbling in the distance. Wyatt was cuddled next to her and they were watching *The Incredibles*, one of his favorites.

He looked up. "Is that God moving his furniture?"

She patted his bottom, but a ribbon of anxiety wrapped around her belly. "Yes, baby. It is."

"Do you think the goats are scared?"

"Nope. I bet Judd has them all snuggled up in the barn."

"And Frank, too?"

"And Frank, too."

"I'm not scared," he said, looking like he might be. "It's just a storm."

"And storms are kind of cool, right?"

He nodded.

Normally she loved Montana's mercurial spring weather, with its brightly lit mornings and afternoon showers. But today she had a heavy feeling she couldn't shake. She was sure it had to do with Judd, with the way they'd left things. But the weather wasn't helping.

"Do you think Maddie's scared?"

"No, honey. I doubt she is."

"Can we call her to make sure?"

She looked down at him, saw how concerned he was, and smiled.

"Okay," she said. "Let's call just to make sure."

Savannah hit Maddie's number on her speed dial, and held Wyatt close as another clap of thunder rattled the dishes in the cupboards.

"Hello?"

"Hey, Maddie. It's Savannah. How are you?"

"I'm good," Maddie said, sounding cheerful. "How are you?"

"Wyatt was just worried about you. He thought you might be scared of the storm, so we wanted to call to check in."

"*Aww.* That's so sweet."

Savannah winked at Wyatt. "So you're doing okay?"

"Yup. I stayed with Luke last night, and we're going to the donut shop this morning. I keep telling him we need to get there before all the sprinkles are gone, but he's still in his pajamas. Hey…Wyatt could come with us!"

Wyatt heard this and lit up. She always worried Maddie would get tired of taking him places, but she seemed to genuinely love it.

"Well, he'd like that a lot, sweetheart. Are you sure it wouldn't be imposing on your time with Luke?"

"No way. He think's Wyatt's the best. And Mary's coming too, so it'll give them more time to stare into each other's eyeballs."

Savannah laughed. "They do that a lot, don't they?"

"Affirmative."

Lighting flashed outside the window and Savannah waited while Wyatt counted underneath his breath.

"One Mississippi, two Mississippi, three Miss—"

The thunder rolled, low and ominous overhead. Savannah felt the smile fade from her lips, thinking again of Judd and the fact that he hadn't answered her calls.

"Honey?" she switched the phone to her other ear. "Have you talked to Judd this morning by any chance?"

"No. Not since he dropped me off last night. Why?"

Swallowing hard, she watched the trees outside bend in the sudden gust of wind. "I don't know. We just…talked after the movie, and didn't really get to finish. I've been calling this morning but he hasn't picked up."

Maddie sighed into the phone. "You mean you had a

fight? It's okay. You can tell me." She sounded like a thera-pist.

"Not really a fight…"

"But he left mad?"

"Not mad. Maybe a little moody."

"Yup, that's Judd. The best way to deal with him when he gets like that is to force him to talk even when he doesn't want to. He can be super stubborn."

"Does he get like this a lot?" she asked, her voice soft.

"Only when it's something he really cares about."

Her heart squeezed.

"Savannah?"

"Yes, honey."

"He's a good guy."

Savannah smiled, looking out at the yard where her rose bushes danced in the wind.

"But if you like him," Maddie continued, "you should know he's also really sad. He tries not to seem that way. And a lot of times he'll hide it by being grumpy, and like this hardened person or something. But he's really just sad. He had to start taking care of us when he was pretty little. And he's never stopped taking care of us. But sometimes I worry he'll always be sad, because nobody ever taught him to be like, softer instead of hard. His dad didn't. My mom was sad too, and she didn't. And now he's like *old* and stuff, and he still won't let anyone teach him to be softer. I think it's because he's scared."

Savannah sat there listening. She didn't know when her eyes had filled with tears, but they had. She blinked, and they spilled down her cheeks. Judd was an amazing man. Loving, kind, generous. But he wasn't perfect. And neither was she. What were the chances that two people, so marred with imperfections, could come together and make something luminous?

She wiped her face with her shirt sleeve. "Maddie, you're a pretty special girl, you know that?"

"My brothers teach me a lot. How to be hard *and* soft. Which I guess sounds weird, but it's true."

"Your brothers are pretty special, too."

"Yup."

Lightning flashed outside the windows, and the lamp flickered. "Can I ask you one more question?"

"Sure."

The ribbon of anxiety squeezing Savannah's belly grew tighter, looping itself around and around again. "What does Judd usually do when he gets sad?"

She was afraid of the answer. Terrified of it, really. But deep down in her heart, in the same place where a brand-new love had finally taken root, she already knew what Maddie was about to say.

"Flying," Maddie whispered with sudden understanding. "He goes flying…"

Chapter Twenty-Two

I T WAS POURING. Savannah leaned forward and gripped the steering wheel, trying her best to see. The rain was coming harder now, in sheets that cascaded down her windshield quicker than the wipers could clear it. Every now and then, electricity would light up the sky, illuminating the angry, billowing clouds overhead, giving her a glimpse inside their heavenly depths.

She'd left Wyatt with Maddie, pulling Luke aside in the other room.

"Don't worry," he'd said, giving her a hug. "He's a good pilot. He wouldn't go up in this."

Still, Savannah had a terrible feeling. She'd also called Tanner, who'd said they'd hauled the Skyhawk out to the airport a few days ago. He'd promised her the same thing, though—Judd would never fly in this weather.

But a voice in the back of her head kept whispering over and over... *The storm was supposed to go around, remember?*

She'd headed straight for the airport, going the back way, which was his route, too. She'd tried calling the hangar, but phone lines were down all over the county. The urge to see him, to have his arms wrapped around her, was growing stronger by the minute. It was more than she could bear, and she didn't know how much of that had to do with wanting to finish their conversation from last night, or how much had to do with needing to see him safe. And on the ground.

As if reading her mind, lightning zigzagged across the sky, pointing like a jagged arrow to the airport in the distance. What if he'd gotten up in the old plane and it had fallen apart or something? She'd heard of tails falling off. Just *falling off* for no apparent reason. And the wind was so strong, it was buffeting her car all over the two-lane highway. She was having trouble driving in a straight line. Just what the hell would that do to a plane a few thousand feet in the air?

She didn't want to know. She just wanted to know Judd was okay. Everything else—the fear of opening up, of getting her heart broken, of being afraid she'd never fully recover—all those things were secondary now. Second to the pull he had over her.

The rain slapped against her windshield in unrelenting waves, blurring the road ahead. Every now and then she'd pass another vehicle, their lights not doing much to cut through the storm, and she'd grasp the wheel harder in an effort to stay in her lane.

Her phone lay beside her on the passenger's seat. Dark and soundless, but at least she still had service. She'd left Judd a message earlier saying she was on her way to the hangar. She'd asked him to wait for her. That she loved him. That she was unsure of all this, too. But that someone had helped her understand they both needed a little softening.

She glanced over at it now, her eyes stinging from lack of sleep. From the tears that kept seeping out, no matter how much she wanted them to stop.

She looked back up just in time to see something in the road. She barely had time to think, barely had time to register. And then her brain caught up with her heartbeat and provided the words...*a deer*... Standing in the wind, soaked by the rain, paralyzed by the headlights.

Instinctively, she swerved, and the car hydroplaned. She was moving in slow motion—the car, the deer, the storm were all moving in slow motion. Somewhere in her mind, images flashed one by one. Wyatt. His sweet smile. The gap between his teeth...

The car skidded into the gravel, and she jerked the steering wheel to the left. She thought of Gran whom she should've gone to see this week, but she'd been busy...

She was airborne, for one second, two seconds, what seemed like an eternity. Her seat belt bit into her neck, but she didn't feel anything. Just the pressure of it stopping her from flying across the front seat as the car flipped on its side. There was the sound of crunching as the car hit something, a fence maybe? And exploded through.

The car skidded, scraped, through grass, mud, water. Her brain kept connecting the dots. She'd been passing a pond. She pictured its black, choppy surface. *Please, God. Don't let me end up in a pond...*

Wyatt, Gran, Mary... All the people she loved. Snapshots behind her eyes, in her heart. And then she saw Judd. Tall and handsome. Rough around the edges, like cut glass.

How she wanted to help him find that softness. That warm, safe place they'd both been looking for, but hadn't been able to find until now.

She cradled her head, trying to protect it if something came through the windshield. She heard screaming, was vaguely aware it was coming from her.

And then the car finally came to a stop. Savannah's heart slammed in her chest. Her ears rang. Her eyes were screwed shut. They fluttered open to mud and grass caked on the windshield.

The car was still on its side, the seat belt the only thing keeping her from dropping headfirst onto the passenger side door. She reached down with trembling hands, held on, and unhooked herself.

Dropping carefully to her feet, she stood on the inside of the door, and pulled in a breath. Then let it out in a shaky whimper. Then pulled in another, and let it out. And over and over again, until her breathing had slowed some.

She reached up and felt her neck, moved her head back and forth to make sure it was still attached. Then looked down, patted her abdomen, wiggled her fingers. She didn't seem to be hurt, thank God. But the realization that she could've died today settled like a brick in her stomach.

Outside, the storm raged. Rain slapped at the car as if angry it was no longer center stage. Lightning flickered and thunder followed. She thought of Judd. *Please let him be safe. Don't let him have gone up in this...*

She bent, looking for her phone. Miraculously, it hadn't gone far. It was lying between the seat and the door, and again, she said a prayer of thanks.

Picking it up, she pressed the home button. She had no idea how far the car had skidded, or if she'd be visible from the road.

All of a sudden, her mind went blank. She had no idea who to call first. Mary? A tow truck? The police? She'd never even had a flat tire before. Her eyes blurred, her heart still pounding from the adrenaline. She shook so much, she could barely make out the numbers on the screen.

Lightning struck again, this time with a sharp clap of thunder right on its tail. Savannah jumped, forcing herself to breathe, waiting for the rumbling to die down before trying to call someone. The lightning was close. Really close. All she could think of was the car acting as a conduit for the electricity in the air. And of Judd's small plane making its way through it.

Somewhere outside, mixed with the low thunder, she thought she heard something. She cocked her head and listened.

Lightning flashed again. Rain pelted the car windows. And she held her breath. *There.* She heard it again. It sounded like someone calling her name.

Frantic, she reached overhead and tried pushing the door open. But it was heavy and would barely budge. With the car being on the sharp angle it was, she'd have to crawl up the seat, and put her foot into the steering wheel to get the leverage to push it open and climb out.

Again. This time she was sure of it. Someone was outside calling her name. Closer this time.

Reaching up, she rolled the window down and stood on her tiptoes.

"Here!" she yelled. "I'm here!"

Thunder clapped. The wind roared in her ears. And then someone was reaching in. *Judd?*

A big hand clamped onto hers. And then she could see his face peering over the window. Handsome, rain soaked, a panicked look in his eyes.

"Jesus Christ, Savannah. Are you okay?"

She nodded, her tears mixing with the rain. She was so relieved to see him. She didn't know until that moment how terrified she'd really been that he was flying when the storm hit.

"Are you hurt?"

"No. There was a deer and I swerved... No, I'm not hurt."

"Hold on. I'm gonna pull you out."

She clung to him as he lifted her up. She scrambled for purchase against the steering wheel and seat back, until she was wriggling out the window with Judd yanking on the back of her jeans, using them as a handle.

He pulled her close and she was immediately enveloped in the warmth from his solid body. He wrapped an arm around her and helped her scoot over the wheel well.

"Careful when you hop down," he said. "It's muddy and the footing is uneven. On three?"

She nodded. The wind snatched at her hair and windbreaker, whipping the hood off to the side like a flag.

"One...two...*three*."

With Judd's arm around her waist, she shimmied off the car and was airborne for a second, before landing with a splash in ankle-deep water.

"Okay?" he asked over the wind, keeping her at an arm's length so he could look her up and down.

"I'm good."

Cold mud oozed into her shoes, soaking her socks. Her toes squished in it.

"Come on. Let's get you to the truck."

Grabbing his hand, she high-stepped through the water, trying not to let the mud suction her tennis shoes off.

Judd's truck sat purring on the side of the road, on the other side of the demolished fence where her car had taken a header. Other than Wyatt being born, and Judd's face peering over the window just now, she didn't think she'd ever seen anything so wonderful in her life.

Hugging herself, she stepped aside while Judd opened the passenger door and helped her in.

The heater was blowing gamely from the dash and Savannah wiped wet tendrils of hair away from her eyes as Judd jogged around to the other side.

He opened the door, the wind howling around the truck, lightning flickering through the heavens.

Climbing in, he pulled it shut again, and all of a sudden the sounds of the storm were muted again. Gentled by the soft, warm cocoon of the cab.

They both sat there for a minute, breathing heavy, soaked to the bone.

Judd reached for her hand, and she grabbed it and

squeezed.

"I thought..." Her voice was froggy, uneven. "I thought you'd gone up in the Skyhawk. I was coming to find you."

"I know. Your texts didn't come through until later. I slept on the couch at the hangar. I'll be honest, I was tempted when the weather was supposed to skirt us. But I'd never fly in anything like this on purpose."

"That's what Luke said. But I just had this terrible feeling. After last night...I couldn't sleep, I kept thinking about you. About us. What you said..."

He rubbed his thumb back and forth over her hand. His skin was rough. But his touch was so incredibly soft. She thought again about those glass edges. Maybe they were already starting to smooth.

"I meant it," he said, his voice low. "The delivery was screwed up. But I love you, Savannah."

She stared at him, her heart pounding out a familiar rhythm. *Judd, Judd, Judd...* "The only thing I could think about last night was how it'd be without you. I made myself imagine it. Walking away from this. Whatever it is. To protect myself and Wyatt from being hurt. But I realized that by trying to protect us all the time, I'm denying us *life*. The really good stuff that sometimes comes with pain. But most of all, it comes with a lot of happiness and joy. Pain is just a by-product of living. A full life."

He smiled. His eyes were especially clear this morning—gray blue, like the ocean after a storm. "So what does that mean? You're willing to give us a shot?"

Rain pelted the roof of the truck, accompanying the

thunder in a song as old as the ages.

She looked down at their fingers. Entwined. She could barely tell where hers ended and his began. When she looked back up, her heart was at peace for the first time in a long, long time. "I am," she said. "Are you?"

"I was driving back to town. Back to your place, when I saw your car. And you were headed for me. I guess that means we were eventually going to find each other, right?"

She nodded.

He leaned close. His eyelashes were dark and spiked with water. Droplets hung from his stubbled jaw. His hair was wet and messy, and she didn't think he'd ever looked so good.

She closed her eyes, anticipating his lips on hers. And then they were there. Moving slowly, gently.

When he pulled away, he cupped her cheek in his palm. One of her favorite things.

"So," he said. "Take it one step at a time?"

"Yes. That."

"Savannah Casteele…will you date me?"

She laughed, the sound mingling with the rain and thunder. And it was a perfect harmony.

"Yes, Judd," she said. "I will date you."

Chapter Twenty-Three

THE COURTYARD OUTSIDE Peggy Morrison's room was just as pretty as Savannah had described. Judd looked around at all the flowers, breathing in their heavy scent. He was no expert on retirement homes, but he could tell this was a good one. Friendly staff, pristine grounds. And most importantly, Peggy seemed really happy—the biggest clue this was a nice place.

He let his gaze settle on her now. She had the same deep green eyes as her granddaughter, the same straight nose and arching brows. But her face was rounder, softened by a white dollop of bangs over her eyes.

Meeting his gaze, she smiled. Her head shook slightly from the Parkinson's, but other than that, she was in great shape, and sharp as a tack. She wore a light sweater, the same color as her cheeks, a flushed rose.

Savannah sat beside her, holding her hand. The afternoon was soft and warm, late July and perfect for iced tea in the shade.

He'd had the opportunity to meet her before this, but honestly, he'd been scared shitless. Because he'd wanted it to go well. He wanted Peggy to like him. He'd never been invited to meet anyone's parents before, or grandparents for that matter, so for Judd, this was a big deal. Inside, he felt like a high schooler, with the nervous palms and thumping heart to match. But there was another reason he was nervous, and that part had everything to do with Savannah.

"I hear Wyatt's follow-up appointment went well?" Peggy asked.

She was trying to coax him into the conversation. He'd been quiet for the last few minutes, lost in thought.

Clearing his throat, he sat forward. "Really well. I think he's their favorite patient of all time."

Savannah beamed.

"I'm not surprised," Peggy said. "He's a superstar. Does he still want to be a cowboy? He'd be the first in the family, I think."

"He does," Savannah said. "But he also wants to wash elephants at the zoo, so…"

"Well, he's got plenty of time to decide. Maybe he can do both."

There was laughter from across the courtyard. They looked over to see Maddie lifting Wyatt up to touch a wind spinner. It was green and blue, and caught the light in hundreds of tiny prisms that moved over the building like fireflies. It looked like one of Savannah's creations, and Judd's heart reacted in that now-familiar way. Swelling uncomfortably inside his chest. Like it might burst if he wasn't careful.

It had taken him a while to get used to that feeling. To acclimate to it. To come to the realization that this was what love felt like. And being careful with it was normal. It meant he had something worth losing.

Peggy looked at him again, this time, her expression softening. She reached out and took his hand. Her skin felt thin, delicate as paper against his.

"I'm so glad you came today," she said. "I know how much you mean to my girl. How kind you've been to her these last few months. You're a good man."

Judd was an expert at pushing messy emotions to the back of his mind. Growing up, it had been a necessity, and one that he'd mastered at an early age.

But there was something about the way Savannah's grandmother was looking at him now. An acceptance that he'd always told himself he didn't need. But that he'd subconsciously craved from the deepest, darkest corners of his being.

He shifted in his wicker chair, and it creaked under his weight. He hoped the damn thing wouldn't snap in half. The hard, little box in his pocket dug into his hip, reminding him to swallow. To breathe. To look into the older woman's eyes and make that newly discovered emotion behave.

"That means…" His voice was gritty, thick. "More than I could explain to you, Ms. Morrison."

She squeezed his hand. "You don't have to explain, son," she said. "I already know."

Savannah was looking at him intently, her pink lips set in a slight frown. She could sense the shift in his thoughts, in his heart. She already knew him that well.

But he knew her, too. He knew she liked jam on her

pancakes instead of syrup. She was ticklish underneath her right arm, but not her left. That she hummed the theme song to *St. Elmo's Fire* when she was in a good mood. And that she would do absolutely anything for her son, and the people she loved.

He was on that list. She loved him. And he loved her.

There were a lot of things that were static, questions that would only be answered over time. But love wasn't going to be a problem for Judd and Savannah. Of that, he was sure. Everything else would fall into place. The look on Peggy's face told him so. The warmth in Savannah's eyes gave him the courage he'd been lacking since the day he'd walked out of his mother's house all those years ago.

Still holding Peggy's hand, he smiled at her, the feeling inside his chest expanding to the point of pain. But it was a good kind of pain. The kind that reminded him what it felt like to really live.

"Truthfully, I should've come sooner," Judd said. "I've been wanting to meet you for a while. I knew you'd be special. You raised Savannah, and she's one of the most amazing women I've ever known. Which makes you especially amazing."

Peggy grinned. Judd felt the warmth of the Montana sun on his shoulders, as mourning doves cooed in the aspen trees a few feet away. The leaves shivered delicately in the summer breeze.

He didn't think he realized until just that moment how glad he was to be back in Marietta. To be raising Maddie here. To be embarking on what might be the best adventure of his life. It was all ahead, like a long, clear runway, stretching out, out, waiting for him to lift into the mountain air and take flight.

Letting go of Peggy's hand, he reached into his pocket. He felt the box there, the velvety promise of it, and pulled it out into the afternoon sunshine.

He heard Savannah take in a breath, heard the laughter of the kids from across the courtyard. The tinkling of windchimes by the windows.

Rubbing his thumb over the box's soft corners, he stared down at it. All the pretense was gone. The walls had finally crumbled away. He was only a man in love.

"I came here today because I wanted to meet you, Ms. Morrison. But also because I wanted to ask for your permission to marry your granddaughter."

He looked up then, his gaze shifting from Peggy, to Savannah. And there, his heart rested. Where it was always meant to be.

"I love you, Savannah," he said. "And I love Wyatt. I know it's soon, but I promise that I'll take care of you both. That I'll love you and cherish you, and we'll be a family. Maybe not a traditional one, but sometimes that's the best kind."

He opened the box and the large diamond solitaire sparkled in the sun. It was his mother's. He knew she would've been happy about this. That her ring would rest on the finger of someone Judd loved. And her memory, the best parts of her, would live on through its brilliance.

Peggy gasped. She caught his gaze and nodded, tears

welling in her eyes.

And then he looked over at Savannah again. For one awful second, he thought she might hesitate. It was fast. A lot of people would question the wisdom of getting engaged so soon. But he didn't care. When it came to Savannah, he didn't want to wait another second. He wanted this. He wanted a future with her.

She held out her hand, her breath coming fast. He pulled the ring from its nesting place in the box and slid it on her finger. A perfect fit.

She looked up, and all the beauty inside her, all the beauty that surrounded her, all the beauty that encompassed her, hit him straight in the chest. Like a white-hot bullet.

"I love you," she said.

"I love you too, baby. Is that a yes?"

Maddie and Wyatt came running up, breathless. The doves continued cooing, oblivious to the world around them. Content in each other, and the promise of long, warm days ahead. They mated for life, a fact Judd only now remembered. A long-forgotten memory floating like a flower on the surface of calm water.

"Yes, Judd," she said, smiling. "That's a yes."

Epilogue

"NO PEEKING, MAMA!"

Judd winked at Wyatt, and motioned for him to keep tugging Savannah along. She held his little hand, grinning from ear to ear. But she kept her promise. Her other hand remained firmly over her eyes.

"Just a little farther," Judd said. "Careful...don't trip."

She looked beautiful today—she wore a yellow sundress that complimented her glowing skin and new curves. Her breasts swelled over the neckline, and her belly swelled underneath the loose fabric. She was six months along, and the doctor thought their baby boy would be big. Ten pounds or more.

Wyatt never got tired of feeling the baby move. Maddie never tired of coming up with names. She was currently on a literary kick, pushing for Peta from *The Hunger Games*. Which made Judd think of a low-carb sandwich, but what did he know?

The barn was warm today, the June sunshine chasing the chill away from the past few weeks. But even on the hottest days, Savannah's new studio would be cool and comfortable. He'd had it built inside the barn, with a chimney for the oven, and its own walls and windows to look out on the stalls that sometimes housed the goats on blustery days. And Frank and her grown ducklings every day in between.

He'd convinced her he'd just been restoring the barn, but even so, he'd had a hell of a time keeping her away.

"Okay, buddy," he said to Wyatt. "You can stop her right there."

Savannah stopped in her tracks, her hand still over her eyes. Her wedding ring sparkled through the dusty light in the barn, a sight that always made his chest constrict.

They'd ended up getting married in Hawaii at his aunt Vivian and uncle Rob's house. It had been a small ceremony, just like Savannah wanted. Maddie, Francie, and Mary had all been her maids of honor, and Peggy had given her away. Wyatt, Tanner and Luke had been Judd's best men, dressed down in linen slacks, Hawaiian shirts, and leis. They'd had a luau on the beach afterward, and danced until the sun lit the Oahu sky in the most brilliant reds, oranges and pinks he'd ever seen.

She'd gotten pregnant almost immediately, and they'd bought the farm. Something Maddie never stopped cracking jokes about. The Tucker place was now the Harlow place. And that filled him with a deep sense of pride. This was his home. This beautiful piece of property was where his family would reside, hopefully for generations to come. He hoped the Tuckers would've liked that. *Life goes on.*

"Can I look now?"

Wyatt came around and leaned into Judd's side. He put his arm around the little boy, holding him close.

"Okay," he said. "You can look."

Savannah took her hand away, her gaze settling on the studio door where a giant blue ribbon hung. There was a plaque beside it that read Wind Spinner Glass Works, the name Savannah had picked out if she ever had a studio of her own. She'd told him one night over dinner—dreamily, as though she'd been holding it close for a really long time.

"Judd."

He grinned. "Yeah."

"A studio?" She stared at him. "My own studio?"

"Yeah, baby."

Her face lit up. Radiating an excitement so profound, he felt it penetrate his own bones. But then her smile faded.

"Your plane," she said. "The Skyhawk. Is this why you sold it?"

He reached for her hand and pulled her to him. She looked like she might cry, and he reached up to rub a thumb along her brow. She cried a lot lately. The baby hormones were wreaking havoc.

"I always thought getting that plane would make me happy. And it did. Just not in the way I'd pictured."

"What do you mean?"

"Selling it meant I could build you a studio. So it did end up making me happy."

"Judd…"

"Nobody needs two planes. I've got the Cessna, and now you've got the studio. This is where you get to make all your beautiful things." He tweaked her nose, then bent to kiss her once, twice. Tasting the cherry gloss on her lips.

In their vows, he'd promised to love her, to keep her safe, to do his best to bring her joy. And now, here they were. On the verge of a lifetime together. And he found that giving her joy was like throwing a boomerang—it came back to him again and again, a thousand times over. All he'd ever had to do was open his heart to the possibility.

Wyatt squeezed his leg. "I'm hungry," he said. "Can we have pancakes for dinner?"

Savannah smiled. "Sure, buddy. I'll make them with Gran's recipe, okay?"

"With extra syrup?"

Judd ruffled Wyatt's baby-fine hair. "With extra syrup," he said. "And jam for your mom."

Savannah wrapped her arms around Judd's neck and stood on her tiptoes. He could feel the firmness of her belly against his hip. The warmth of her breath against his neck.

"I love you, Captain Harlow," she said. "Have I told you that lately?"

"Once or twice. Does this mean you'll finally let me take you flying?"

"You've already taken me flying," she said softly. "To the moon and back."

The End

The Harlow Brother Series

The Harlow brothers learned at a young age that family is what you make of it. Born on the wrong side of the tracks and abandoned by their father, Judd, Luke and Tanner have grown into remarkably tough men who are jaded by life. But when they come together as guardians of their orphaned half-sister, they'll find that love is what you make of it, too. As they learn how to be the fathers they never had, their carefully constructed walls begin to crack. But it will take three strong women to tear those defenses down for good, and show them what true happiness looks like.

Book 1: *Tanner's Promise*

Book 2: *Luke's Gift*

Book 3: *Judd's Vow*

Available now at your favorite online retailer!

About the Author

For Kaylie Newell, storytelling is in the blood. Growing up the daughter of two gifted writers, she knew eventually she'd want to follow in their footsteps. While she's written short stories her whole life, it wasn't until after her kids were born that she decided to shoot for the moon and write her first romance novel. She hasn't looked back since!

Kaylie lives in Southern Oregon with her husband, two little girls, two indifferent cats and a mutt named Pedro.

Visit Kaylie at KaylieNewell.com

Thank you for reading

Judd's Vow

If you enjoyed this book, you can find more from all our great authors at TulePublishing.com, or from your favorite online retailer.

TULE
PUBLISHING

Made in the USA
Monee, IL
28 December 2020

55797447R00132